Ex Utero

LAURIE FOOS

A Harvest Book

Harcourt Brace & Company

San Diego　　New York　　London

for Michael

Requests for permission to make copies of any part of the
work should be mailed to: Permissions Department,
Harcourt Brace & Company, 6277 Sea Harbor Drive,
Orlando, Florida 32887-6777.

Library of Congress Cataloging-in-Publication Data
Foos, Laurie, 1966–
Ex utero/Laurie Foos. — 1st Harvest ed.
p.   cm. — (A Harvest book)
ISBN 0-15-600464-X
1. Women — Physiology — Fiction.   2. Uterus — Fiction.
3. Human reproduction — Fiction.   I. Title.
[PS3556.0564E95   1996]
813'.54 — dc20   96-25902

Text set in Electra
Designed by Lydia D'moch

Printed in the United States of America
First Harvest edition 1996
A C E D B

HARVEST AMERICAN
Writing

Ex Utero

ONE

Rita is lying in bed one night when she realizes she's lost her uterus. She does not remember its falling out of her, like change out of an overstuffed wallet. Her ambivalent feelings about having children, she thinks, may have caused the womb to shrink away and fall out of her like a kind of discharge, an escape from lack of use. Her stomach constricts with the empty feeling of fruitlessness, a dry rot inside her that she has felt since coming home from the shopping mall. It was at the mall, she believes, that her womb fell out and was lost in the crowd, in a mob of women with baby strollers, their feet stomping over her last shot at motherhood.

She thinks that the mall is the last place she felt whole, that somewhere between the shoe store and the lingerie counter of a major department store, her uterus had somehow fallen out. There she'd bought red high heels and a low-slung bra, a series of opaque pantyhose to match every outfit she owns. Somehow, in her quest to achieve a versatile wardrobe, she'd lost her womb, the way some people misplace car keys or a pair of eyeglasses.

"Good God, George!" she screams, jumping from the bed with her hands over her stomach, "my uterus is gone!"

George rolls over in bed and switches on the overhead light. He is accustomed to being assaulted during the night by his high-strung wife. Frequently she wakes him after especially vivid dreams and acts them out for him in their bedroom; he is always required to play a part. Tonight he must be the savior, she says, and hands him a flashlight to search for her lost womb.

"It was in there the last time I checked," she says to her abdomen with a look of distraction. "Now it could be anywhere."

George is certain the womb is somewhere inside the apartment, he tells her with the degree of authority he thinks befits his role as savior. She is careless, he thinks, but has a certain level-headedness that he has always loved.

"I simply refuse to believe that you tossed it away in a mall like a battered penny," he says with a hint of bitterness. "It must've fallen out somewhere in our very own home."

Together they get down on their hands and knees to search under the bed, in the bedroom closets, in Rita's underwear drawer. George even pads into the bathroom and searches inside the toilet, lifting the porcelain lid and jiggling the handle. Rita does not know why he links her uterus so closely with the toilet, but she agrees that they should leave no stone unturned.

They move into the kitchen and tear apart the pantry, tipping over tins of spoiled tuna in the refrigerator and jars of grape jelly with sticky film over the lids. Rita opens a carton of eggs and searches the back of the refrigerator for clues. In her haste she drops an egg on the floor, the shell landing with a splat and the bright yellow liquid seeping over the tile.

It is then that she begins to weep.

"I know I had it before I bought these shoes," she says, pointing between sobs to the pair of red heels she'd bought that day. She thinks about how she bought the heels as a turn-on for George, how he loves to see her feet squeezed tightly into red high heels. How she had gone on to buy a matching red teddy with a crotchless red heart, had even tried on the outfit in the ladies' dressing room. George tries to comfort her, but she cannot stop crying, smearing the spilled egg with her hands.

"Perhaps I should have quit while I was ahead," she says. She notices pointedly that George is without an erection, even with the red shoes so close by.

She thinks about her day at the mall, about the rows of shining red shoes and the difficulty of choosing a pair, the mothers and their strollers with babies straining against harnesses. How grateful she was that she was not one of those, with a diaper bag and a blouse stained with drool, breasts that would no longer sit peacefully in the cups of bras. How could you wear heels with a baby in tow, she'd wondered, feeling a stab of pity for the mothers and their tired flat loafers. A feeling sinks in her stomach; she licks the remains of the egg from her fingers and weeps.

"We'll find it," he says, persuading her to go back to bed and dream about where she's lost it. Her dreams are so vivid, after all, he tells her. Maybe she'll see it there on the floor of the mall, dented from the foot of a careless shopper. "Someone will have seen it and handed it in to the lost and found," he says, and spreads his arms out like a true savior.

She nods, but inside she senses that even if another woman finds the uterus, she might never get it back. The sight of a healthy womb lying in a crowded mall might drive a woman to do something out of the ordinary. Rita now knows what it's like to be without a womb, and does not know what she herself is capable of. She clasps her hands over the emptiness of her middle and thinks about how she might get her uterus back. For the first time since she was fourteen, when she first started to menstruate, she does not dream.

Rita thinks about how she managed to spend the entire day at the mall without realizing she'd lost her uterus. She'd seen an old man jerking off outside the shoe store and decided to buy the red heels in the window. She'd thought about the way the shoes had turned the old man on, hoping they'd have the same effect on George. That night when she'd felt George press his hairy thigh into hers, she realized that she'd lost her uterus.

How she lost it was another matter. She feels sure that if it had slid down her pantyhose she would have felt it. If she had passed it in the ladies' room, she would have heard the splash of its hitting the toilet water. And if it had fallen out in the car, she'd have seen it there in all its glory, pink and full of hope, against the dull blue vinyl of the driver's seat.

In the morning, she calls the security division of the shopping mall to make a report. George says it is best to tell the story as clearly as she remembers it, not to color the facts with embarrassment or lack of candor.

"Your only hope of recovery," George says, looking pale on his way out the door, "is not to hold back."

The man on the other end of the phone asks her to provide him with a suitable description. He breathes heavily, his breath like static through the receiver. She sits in her bathrobe wearing the new red heels; the stark whiteness of her bare legs against the thrill of the heels brings a lump to her throat.

"What exactly does a uterus look like?" he says, his voice low in her ear, intrigued.

She feels herself blushing, although she knows he can't see her, and tightens her grip on the telephone cord. She thinks about what it might look like, fleshless and clear, a symbol of the lack of color in her life. But she prefers to think of it as pink and swelled to bursting, its fluid shimmering under the lights of the mall.

She clears her throat.

"I don't know," she says, her voice becoming high and breathless. "I only know that it's mine."

The man takes a deep breath; she can hear the voices of the people at the mall. *We told you so*, they seem to say. *You women are all alike.*

The man asks for her address and a credit card number. He can offer no promises, he says, perhaps a gift certificate as compensation. Perhaps next time she might be more careful, he says, and hangs up before she can respond.

That night she drives to the mall in her new red

heels and stands at the top of the escalator. A group of women are standing at the bottom eating apples and comparing receipts. Rita watches them, feeling the terrible emptiness in her middle, the warmth of the shoes on her feet. Any day they could lose their wombs, too, she wants to warn them, but thinks it is a lesson that they had best learn for themselves.

"Has anyone seen my uterus?" she screams to the people below. She thinks of the egg smashed on her kitchen floor and fights back the tears. Several of the women whisper to each other and hold their hands proudly over their own stomachs.

"I'm glad I'm not in her shoes," she hears one of them say. When no one answers she rides the escalator down and takes out her flashlight, the beam of light in front of her as she prepares to search the mall for her lost womb.

On the third day the phone calls begin. George tries twice to make love to her but tells her the thought of her womb out in the world somewhere so cold and life-less kills his erection every time.

"We've got to get it back" is all he will say, his

limp penis resting in his hand, curled up like a bad memory.

Rita has drawn pictures of the way she imagines her uterus might look and she drafts posters to be tacked up throughout the neighborhood. A soft blush like good wine in a small kidney-shaped cartoon. *If found, please call*, she writes in large block letters. *Owner desperate.*

That night the telephone rings. She is sitting at the kitchen table with George eating scrambled eggs and not talking. She rubs one of the red heels against George's bare leg, but he stiffens at her touch. She swallows the eggs and tries not to weep.

George answers the phone on the first ring.

"Hello?" he says, his mouth full of scrambled eggs, yellow bits of egg clinging to the sides of his mouth. Rita washes her eggs down with a glass of milk and waits.

"It's for you," he says, and hands her the receiver.

She holds the phone to her ear and waits for the person to speak. The red shoes squeeze around the tops of her feet, suffocating her heels.

"Lady," the man says, his voice dark and scratchy, "what if I told you I found your uterus?"

Rita feels her stomach squeeze, chokes on the last bit of eggs.

"I'm not saying I have it," the man says, "but what if?"

She reaches for George's hand, but he turns away from her and begins scraping the remains of his eggs into the wastebasket.

"If you had it," she says, trying not to sound anxious, "then I'd ask you to kindly give it back."

The man laughs, a throaty rasp that makes her breath catch in her throat. George rinses the plates. She feels her throat tighten as pieces of egg spiral down the drain.

"C'mon, lady," he says, "you can do better than that."

He hangs up before she has a chance to respond.

That night she and George try again to make love. She lies on her back with her ankles around his waist while he tries to enter her. She insists on wearing the red heels, although he begs her not to. Again and again she feels his limp penis squished against her, the red shoes shining in the air above his back.

"It's no use," he says, gazing mournfully at her feet. "I simply can't get inside."

She pretends not to notice as he climbs off her and takes out a drawing pad and crayon. He sits on the bedroom floor and draws cartoons of their thwarted lovemaking, an oversize penis trying to squeeze itself into a wombless woman. She dangles her feet in the air and tries to ignore the emptiness in her middle.

The telephone rings while George is tracing his penis with a red magic marker. Rita runs into the kitchen, tripping over her heels in an effort to reach it on the first ring.

"Have you found my uterus?" she says, her voice barely a whisper.

The man on the other end laughs. She removes the red heels and throws them in the corner of the room.

"So what if I did?" he says, and hangs up before she can answer. She stands there for a long time listening to the dial tone, the receiver hanging over her shoulder. Just like someone holding an infant, she thinks.

After a week Rita goes back to the mall to return the red heels. Perhaps it is her own vanity, she thinks, that has caused her to misplace her uterus. Even if she doesn't find her womb, perhaps George's erections will return once the red heels are gone.

"They're just too full of life," he'd said, when she asked him why he didn't like the red heels, "against the backdrop of your barren self."

Several stores have posted her signs in their plate-glass windows. There is the drawing of her uterus against the background of mannequins wearing costume jewelry. Another with a series of faceless mannequins with red hair and low-cut brassieres. She places the red heels on the counter and asks the sales-girl if anyone has reported finding the uterus of a thirty-one-year-old woman.

"Not that I know of," the salesgirl says, with a hint of a smile playing at the corners of her lips. Rita blushes; even she can see that the girl has fertility written all over her face.

On her way out of the mall Rita gets down on her hands and knees, feeling along the coldness of the tile. Her life has gone to hell in a handbasket, she thinks, her lacquered nails scraping over the floor. When she is about to give up, a woman with a stroller comes barreling toward her, the wheels running over Rita's hands.

"For God's sake, can't you see how low I've sunk?" she screams at the woman. But the woman doesn't stop, she and her baby laughing at Rita as they round the corner on two wheels.

One of the men from mall security comes and helps her to her feet.

"You've got to be careful, lady," the man says, his eyes round and full of concern. "Anything can happen at the mall."

In a whisper she asks him if he'd direct her to the nearest shoe store. Nothing would make her feel better, she tells him, than a new pair of red high heels.

After several more attempts at lovemaking, Rita and George decide to forgo sex for nights of public television. If they can no longer connect in the bedroom, George says, then perhaps they might achieve some intimacy during a series of documentaries. Rita makes bowls of popcorn and wears the red heels day after day as a symbol of her commitment to not give up her search.

_____

One night while George watches a program on child-birth, Rita decides to take more drastic measures. On a whim she calls an 800 number and places an ad for a missing person. Although the man on the telephone argues that the service is for people and not for organs or objects, he says that the desperation in her voice seems genuine enough to bend the rules in her case.

"I've never met a woman who lost her womb before," he tells her, his voice full of longing. "How does it feel?"

She looks over at George, who sits stroking his limp penis and eating handfuls of popcorn.

"It feels," she says, "like my life is over."

"We'll find it," he says, earnestly. "That's what we're here for."

She hears a catch in his voice, as if the man is fighting back tears.

Rita hangs up just as the woman on television is beginning to bear down, the vagina opening huge and red, the womb straining to free the baby and send it out into the world. George reaches over and holds her hand. Neither of them says anything when the woman begins to scream.

The ad for Rita's womb runs for several weeks. Her name flashes on the screen in large pink letters, a hotline number running along the bottom of the large picture.

> WOMB, APPROXIMATELY THIRTY-ONE YEARS OLD. NEVER BEEN PREGNANT. LAST SEEN AT AREA SHOPPING MALL NEAR REYNOLDS' SHOES. BELIEVED TO BE PINK AND ABOUT THE SIZE OF A MAN'S FIST. ANYONE WHO HAS SEEN THIS WOMB OR HAS ANY INFORMATION, PLEASE CALL LOCAL AUTHORITIES.

George tapes the ad on the VCR and begins playing it for hours at a time. The sight of the ad on the screen with the description of the womb inflames him, he says. He holds Rita down on the floor and thrusts his limp penis against her over and over until she begs him to stop. They sit on the floor and eat popcorn, watching the ad frozen on the television, but the phone does not ring.

A group of women appear at Rita's door after the ad has run several times. They are dressed in black and wear open-toed sandals. Rita opens the door for them and feels self-conscious in her high red heels, her face flushed from sitting so close to the television and dreaming of her uterus.

They sit down at Rita's kitchen table and eat unsweetened low-fat plain yogurt. They say they are an organization called the Fruitless Wombs, which is devoted to women's causes, and that her cause is one of the most poignant they've ever heard of. Rita laps at her yogurt and catches sight of George watching them from the living room with a frightening erection. She is close to tears.

"We're a political group," says the leader, a woman with high cheekbones and wire-rimmed glasses. "We can get you national exposure, a live spot on television."

George strokes his erection furiously, rolls his eyes with pleasure. Rita crosses her legs, the women staring down at the red heels. She tries not to stare at his erection, thinks about the days when she still had her uterus, the nights of lovemaking, the feeling of being whole.

"I don't want to be a celebrity," she tells them shyly. "I just want my uterus back."

She hears George groaning in the other room, the

harsh sounds of his breath. She lets the yogurt swirl around on her tongue. The women excuse themselves, tell her they have other appointments to keep, other wombs to retrieve.

"How does it feel," one woman whispers on her way out the door, "to know you're a symbol of infertility?"

She has no answer. Instead she thanks the women for their time and says that she looks forward to meeting with them again. Afterward she sinks against the door and hears George panting. She runs into the living room to take advantage of his erection, but his penis has wilted again, his hand full of semen. She holds her hands over her stomach and begins to weep. George puts his arms around her, tries to apologize for the excitement that has overtaken him.

"Those women had wombs," he says, his voice low. "I just couldn't stop myself."

Rita spends the night staring at the ad for her lost uterus. She thinks about the women, about their penchant for yogurt and George's erection. She watches the words passing over the screen. NEVER BEEN PREGNANT, it says, the words flashing on the television, larger and larger until they threaten to fill up the room.

TWO

Harry, a security guard at the local mall, eats his cereal every morning in front of the television set. He has not had sex in three years, ever since his girlfriend Adele told him she no longer liked the feel of him pulsing against her at night. She'd had nightmares about his erections, she said, and could no longer live under the stiff shadow of his penis stalking her through her life.

"I see it in my dreams and have it in me at night," she'd said when she packed her belongings in plastic bags and moved out. "I simply need some rest."

Harry takes a long time with his breakfast. At the mall

he often has to skip lunch to chase women with baby strollers stuck on the escalator or to stop old men from jerking off in front of the shoe stores. It is the sight of the red heels that gets them, Harry thinks, with his hand on his zipper and the milk running down his throat.

He is watching the cable station when he sees the ad for the lost uterus. For the past several weeks he's taken to watching the cable ads to avoid erotic stimulation. On every other channel he is assaulted by pantyhose ads, ads for high-heeled shoes, or those long commercials about feminine hygiene spray. He does not like to jerk off and he misses his girlfriend, a fact which is evident in the near-constant erection that strains against the zipper of his mall security uniform.

WOMB, APPROXIMATELY THIRTY-ONE YEARS OLD. NEVER BEEN PREGNANT. LAST SEEN AT AREA SHOPPING MALL NEAR REYNOLDS' SHOES. BELIEVED TO BE PINK AND ABOUT THE SIZE OF A MAN'S FIST. ANYONE WHO HAS SEEN THIS WOMB OR HAS ANY INFORMATION, PLEASE CALL LOCAL AUTHORITIES.

Harry stiffens in his seat, nearly chokes on a mouthful of cereal in the heavy milk. As head of mall security, he is incensed that a case this big has slipped by right under his nose. Why hasn't he been informed of a loss as great as this? He zips up his fly and tosses his bowl of cereal into the sink. When he gets to work, he thinks, with a toughness he hasn't felt in years, heads will roll.

Outside the mall a group of women in black open-toed sandals are holding up signs and humming low, haunting melodies. *Mall Unsafe for Women*, some of the signs say. *Wombs Beware*. Harry puts on his security cap and approaches the women. Already he can feel the erection straining at his pants.

"Where were you," one of the women screams, shaking her fist in Harry's face, "when that poor woman lost her womb right under your nose?"

Harry blushes; in a meek voice he asks the women to please confine their protests to the parking lot.

"There are shoppers in there," he pleads. "Have some respect."

Inside the mall Harry calls his fellow security guards to a mall-wide meeting. Why wasn't he told, he demands, holding his hat over his erection, about a matter as delicate as this one? The other men hang their heads sheepishly and offer tenuous explanations.

"Frankly, Chief," one of the younger men says, "I wouldn't know a womb if I stepped right over it."

Harry clasps his hands tighter on the rim of his hat. He cannot stop the image of the ad running in his mind. NEVER BEEN PREGNANT. The words flash over and over again in his mind. He is amazed to find he does not think of his girlfriend, but instead imagines a woman standing naked in front of him wearing only a pair of red high heels.

One guard steps forward and takes Harry by the arm. He explains how he got a call from a woman several weeks before who claimed to have lost her womb in the mall. He thought it was run-of-the-mill, he tells Harry, some hysteric who's realized she can no longer have kids. Think of all the calls they get, he says. Lost keys, lost kids, a frantic husband searching desperately for his shopaholic wife. Perhaps the job is getting to Harry.

"I'll tell you one thing, though, Chief," he says in Harry's ear. "I had a hard-on for three days."

Harry glares at the man, feels his own erection stabbing at the polyester uniform pants. It is their duty to find the woman's womb. He imagines the wombless woman floating above the mall in red heels, coming to sit with him in the mornings while he eats his cereal and watches the cable ads. He has never felt more alone.

"You two check all the ladies' bathrooms, you search the maternity stores, and I," he says, trying to conceal his longing, "will stand guard at the shoe store."

The men disperse, hurrying to their respective posts with erections in their pants. Harry hurries to the shoe store, where he stands in the doorway, hoping to get a glimpse of the woman coming back to the store for her womb. The salesgirl nods to him and offers him a glass of water; he feels his throat tightening at the sight of her fertile body, thinks of how the poor woman must have felt, her own body emptied of promise.

"No, thank you," he says, and is surprised to find he is fighting back tears. He has not felt this moved since Adele told him she could no longer bear his erections.

At five o'clock he lingers at the shoe store, though it is the end of his shift. A woman approaches the store in a white dress and a pair of red heels, her dark hair tied in a knot at the nape of her neck. The young salesgirl begins to lower the gate for closing time, smiles at the woman, and says good-night to Harry.

"We're closing," she says, and locks the gate without looking at him.

The woman's face squinches up in pain, and she gazes longingly at a pair of red stiletto heels that Harry thinks are probably out of the woman's price range. He feels his heartbeat quickening in his chest, the ad for the lost womb flashing in his head.

"Is it you?" he says, laying a hand on her arm, the feel of her cool white flesh sending a shock through him.

But the woman shakes her head, pulls her arm away in a huff.

"Jesus," she says, "can't a woman even buy a pair of shoes these days?"

Harry walks through the mall with his head down. The men hurry over to him, tell him in concerned voices that the womb still has not been found.

"We won't give up, Chief," one of the men says. "You can count on us."

Harry nods, waving his hand at them in dismissal. On the way out he sees an old man jerking off in front of one of the shoe stores, but he no longer has the strength to stop him.

THREE

Rita begins a series of appearances on syndicated talk shows. The Fruitless Wombs have not reneged on their promise; they book interviews for her on all of the major networks.

"This is an issue that is crying out to be heard," the leader of the group tells her, "and you are our designated spokeswoman."

When she tells George about her plans to appear on the programs, he cannot hide his contempt. For several days he hangs black-and-white drawings of his erection on the refrigerator as a reminder of what they once shared.

"A lost womb is not a cause," he tells her at the kitchen table, piling broken eggshells on his plate. "It's the destruction of our life."

Later Rita sweeps the eggshells into the garbage when George isn't looking. While he is asleep she tears down the drawings and crumples them into balls. She has a life without his erection, she wants to tell him, but instead she leaves him a note.

Dear George,
I have thought long and hard about losing your erections, and have realized, after great pain, that I may be able to live without them. My womb, however, is another story. If I must be a symbol of other women's suffering, then so be it. I'm off to The Nodderman Show.

Love,
Rita

Backstage Rita is prepped by make-up personnel and script coordinators. Try to say *womb*, they coach her. *Uterus* is far too clinical. They dress her in a sharp red suit and white blouse, a pair of matching red heels. Rod

Nodderman, the host of the show, gives her a squeeze before they go on the air, his white hair tickling the side of her cheek.

"I've never hugged a woman who lost her womb before," he chuckles. "This is a new experience."

On stage Rita is joined by a panel of gynecologists, an expert on menopause, and a well-known sex therapist. She tells Nodderman in a stage whisper that questions about her husband are off-limits, and he gives her a knowing look. He tells her to keep her hands pressed to her stomach and to look at the camera with longing.

"There are women out there who can learn from you," he says. "Don't let them make the same mistake."

At home George gathers up the drawings of his lost erection and reads Rita's note. Despite himself, he tunes into *The Nodderman Show* and is shocked at the sight of Rita onstage, her face stark against the redness of her suit. During a commercial the telephone rings. He forces himself to answer it.

"How does it feel to live with a symbol?" a man asks him.

George hangs up to the sound of laughter, the strains of Nodderman's theme song blaring over the television.

"There are several theories as to why this woman has lost her womb," a gynecologist explains. "First off, she is married and childless; the pressure to procreate may often have severe physical side effects," he continues, "as evident here in the womb simply falling out and refusing to perform. Just closing up shop, if you will."

Rita holds her hands tightly over her stomach. She thinks of the women in the mall, the crowds of babies while she tried on pairs of shoes. She holds her hand up for the camera to see; there is a stroller-tire mark across the length of her hand.

Nodderman reaches over and takes Rita's hand. Without meaning to, she finds herself looking to see whether or not he has an erection. But Nodderman knows what she's after and instructs the cameraman to shoot him only from the waist up. During a commercial break, he presses his fingers into the stroller mark on her hand.

"You women are all alike," he says, with a kind of reverence in his voice.

Rita hears a baby crying in the audience. She feels the urge to grab Nodderman by the ears and straddle him right there on the stage, but restrains herself with the little control she has left. She can feel him looking at the red heels. The baby will not stop crying.

A commercial for Cheerios appears on George's screen, tiny circles with milk sopping through their openings. A girl in her mid-teens holds the spoon and slips it into her ripe open mouth. George cannot stop masturbating, although he fails to achieve an erection.

During the break, the producer instructs Nodderman to prime the audience. He can smell the wombs in the audience, he tells Nodderman, with a terrifying smile on his face. There is a sense of ripeness, Nodderman agrees, that he has not felt before. Rita smells her own rot.

When Nodderman isn't looking, she adjusts her stockings and lifts one of her feet into the camera's line of vision. She poises the foot in the air and whispers a message behind Nodderman's back.

"George," she mouths, "can't you see I've lost my womb?"

There is a humming in the audience, the low sucking noises of a baby being nursed in the third row. One of the gynecologists on the panel turns to Rita and points an accusing finger at her.

"Plenty of women have been deprived of their wombs," he says, his voice shaking. "But yours has been lost like an old suitcase in an airport."

The women in the audience rise to their feet and shake their fists at the gynecologists. They have reached a fever pitch; even the Fruitless Wombs cannot control them, although they try to, pounding their sandals into the carpet in a call for order. An eighty-year-old woman in the front row collapses in a fit of hot flashes, which she has not experienced in nearly thirty years. Nodderman rushes to her with his microphone in hand, but she can only pant and clutch at her breast like a stage actress. In desperation Nodderman turns to a pregnant woman in the last row to restore a sense of calm to the show. Rita gasps as the woman reaches for the microphone with her pale hand.

"What does your womb mean to you?" Nodderman screams, thrusting the microphone against her swollen belly.

For a moment Rita hears the thumping of the fetal heartbeat through the sound system and twists her feet in anguish. The red heels threaten to squeeze the blood out of her feet and ankles. She imagines herself pinned to the stage with the red heels cemented to the ground. Her only way out is to grab Nodderman by the crotch of his pants and beg for mercy. She thinks of George and his lost erections, the deflation of their lives.

"My womb," says the pregnant woman, looking straight at Rita, her eyes round and full of hope, "is everything I am."

The camera closes in on Nodderman sitting at the foot of the stage to Rita's left, the red heels suspended in the space behind Nodderman's head. He sniffs in the air and motions to the producer.

"Do you smell something rotting?" he says, and runs his hand through the thick white hair. The producer signals to him that time is running out.

"To our viewers at home," he says, standing and taking Rita's hand, "I ask you this. Have pity on this poor woman. Find her womb. Imagine yourself in her shoes."

The audience is silent.

While the final credits are rolling, Rita beseeches the cameraman to run the ad for her lost womb. Before the end of the credits, the phones are ringing off the hooks.

"Are you there, caller?" Nodderman says just before the station identification.

The man, who wishes to be known only as Harry, head of security at a local shopping mall, asks to speak directly to Rita, but the producer orders him to say his piece on the air.

"If it's good enough for her," the producer says, "it's good enough for the American people."

But there is only the sound of his heaving breath in the final seconds before the screen turns black.

Afterward Rita shakes Nodderman's hand and thanks him for his hospitality. He is not without a kind heart, she notes. She could see his erection straining in his pants during the pregnant woman's speech. It is a moment, she says, that she will not soon forget. The audience claps wildly, and one woman holds her baby up in a salute.

Nodderman removes the microphone from his lapel and stares at the red heels.

"It's a man's world," he says, looking strangely sheepish. Rita nods; she is not unmoved.

At home she finds George standing naked in the kitchen with his feet squeezed inside an old pair of her high heels. All of his drawings have been crumpled and hang deliberately out of the wastebaskets like flags at half-mast. She offers to make him a helping of scrambled eggs, but he holds up a plastic bag full of his clothes.

"You looked good on camera," he says, "even without the womb."

They fall on the floor together and try desperately to make love, but again he cannot achieve an erection. Instead they lie on the floor and rub their feet together furiously until the sides of the heels begin to wear away, the color fading into smatterings of pale scuff marks.

FOUR

Adele likes to make love with her boyfriend Leonard while watching talk shows. There is something about the distant murmur of voices, she says, that never fails to propel her to orgasm. Some of the syndicated shows do the trick, but it is *The Nodderman Show* that drives her into a frenzy. Certain shows have sent her tearing at Leonard's hair and begging for commercials. She has been known to scream with pleasure at the opening strains of game show theme songs, writhing on the bed from the spinning of the Wheel of Fortune. But it is the shock of Nodderman's white hair that mounts a fury in her loins, she says; no man alone can hope to match it.

Leonard is not averse to talk shows and even thrills to the epithets Adele screams during Nodderman's more poignant moments. At times Adele has found him trying to conceal his erection during the theme song; it is a genuine aphrodisiac. Her former boyfriend, Harry, on the other hand, had insisted on turning the sound down and wearing his mall security hat, which blocked her view of the television set. During their lovemaking she had yanked off his hat and strained to see the television, but he had urged her head closer to him, keeping her from seeing the screen. Although she had a deep affection for Harry, she could no longer live without the sight of Nodderman's hair to pull her through her roughest moments.

She is not sure whether her actual leaving is what hurt Harry so deeply, or whether he simply could not bear up under the strict standards for manhood that Nodderman had set. At the end of their relationship he'd begged her to wear a pair of red heels he'd bought wholesale at the mall and to turn off the television for good. For three nights she wore the heels and swore off *Nodderman* to try to save the relationship. But then she began to equate a blank television screen with the ferocity of his erections. The sight of the television without the grace of Nodderman parading across the screen made her think of an enormous penis that threatened to fill up her entire body. She had nightmares about the shadow of his penis looming on the ceiling above her bed, stabbing at her unconscious mind. Living without Nodderman was like having a penis inside her day and night. It was a sacrifice, ultimately, that she was unwilling to make.

One afternoon Adele and Leonard enjoy a prolonged round of foreplay in the minutes before *The Nodderman Show*. Adele prepares for the excitement of the show, wears a tight black teddy with the crotch cut out in the shape of a heart, edged in bright red thread. Today's guest, the announcer says during a commercial, will be a woman who apparently lost her womb in a local shopping mall. Adele is also childless, and feels a pull of affection for the woman before actually seeing her face on the screen. She and Leonard grab and kiss each other with an urgency they haven't felt since Nodderman's sweeps week.

The woman appears on the screen in a pair of red heels and a matching suit, her hair coiled back in a bun and a look of such emptiness in her eyes that Adele feels a sympathetic tightness in her own middle. The woman is in her early thirties and is now wombless, Nodderman says, which elicits a low murmur of sadness from the audience.

Leonard runs his tongue around the crotchless red heart. Adele strains forward to get a better look at the woman, to see the red heels on the poor woman's feet. She thinks of the many days she and Leonard have spent screwing in front of *The Nodderman Show* while this poor woman has searched frantically for her womb. For the first time since she'd begun tuning in to *The Nodderman Show*, she feels distracted, even guilty, about Leonard's lovemaking.

"Are you there, caller?" she hears Nodderman say as Leonard mounts her, poised above her just before his entry.

There is a long close-up of the woman's face on the TV screen, her eyes closed with longing, then the camera pans the audience. A woman in the front row pounds her breast in protest. In the distance there is the low sound of a baby suckling at its mother's breast.

Then Adele feels a terrible squeezing between her legs, and hears a clapping sound like a door being shut. The caller breathes, the volume on the television growing louder and louder.

"My God," she says aloud, "it's Harry."

Leonard thrusts against her again and again, but she feels nothing. He simply cannot enter her, he says, holding his penis out before her like a sword. She opens her legs wider, revealing the lace of the crotchless heart, but her body simply refuses to receive him. When Nodderman goes to a commercial, they scramble off the bed for a mirror.

In the bathroom Adele holds the mirror between her legs and gasps. It is as if her vagina has disappeared, she says, shut itself up like a steel trap. The folds of skin are gone, the opening closed over with her own flesh, like a slab of cement over a basement door. She stabs at the flesh with her fingernails, but there is no entry at all, not even a hint of where the opening had once been.

"Good Lord, Leonard," she says, "it's simply closed up shop."

Leonard gets down on his knees and examines it for himself. Then he prods at it with his penis, thrusting his hips until he is sweating. Adele gets up from the toilet and runs back into the bedroom. Nodderman's theme song blares over the television set, Leonard's huge erection follows Adele to the bed. He punches at the vagina with his fist, but it refuses to open, even during the final credits.

After a time they lie on opposite sides of the bed and pant. If she closes her eyes she can hear Harry breathing, and see the woman from the show dangling her red high heels in the camera's eye. She hears car doors slamming, one after another, locks being turned in the apartments next door. She switches to the cable channel and tries to catch her breath.

WOMB, APPROXIMATELY THIRTY-ONE YEARS OLD. NEVER BEEN PREGNANT. LAST SEEN AT AREA SHOPPING MALL NEAR REYNOLDS' SHOES. BELIEVED TO BE PINK AND ABOUT

THE SIZE OF A MAN'S FIST. ANYONE WHO
HAS SEEN THIS WOMB OR HAS ANY INFOR-
MATION, PLEASE CALL LOCAL AUTHORITIES.

She thinks about the shoes that Harry had bought her at the mall, about the woman in her red heels and the sheer power of her story. How lying there on her back with Leonard above her, careful not to block her view, she had seen the woman's face twisted with anguish, the sounds of Harry's breathing coming over the television set. How she could no longer feel the burning that the *Nodderman* theme song had once set off within her.

"You women are all alike," she hears Nodderman say. The woman with her lost womb holds her hands out to the audience in a gesture that begs for sympathy.

Nodderman does not know, Adele thinks, how terribly right he is.

That night Leonard makes a trip to the hardware store for a hammer and chisel, a set of pliers and a drill. There is not yet call for worry, he says. He is a carpenter, after all, and can fix most any problem. Adele walks around the apartment in her old pair of red heels and weeps, her sealed vagina scraping against the crotch of her pants.

While Leonard is gone she makes herself a plate of scrambled eggs as a consolation. The sound of Harry's breath reverberates in her ears, his deep sighs filling her with images of his penis throwing shadows on the walls of her living room. For a time she sits at the kitchen table and eats her scrambled eggs. Out of desperation she switches off the television set, but she finds even the silence distracting.

When Leonard returns, Adele, who has changed into a black lace crotchless teddy, lies spread-eagled on the sofa, her red heels dangling over its arms. Leonard lays his tools down on the hardwood floor, takes out a tape measure, and begins jotting down dimensions. A chip to the left, some heavy chiseling in the center, perhaps a drill will do, he says. He draws a diagram of Adele's body on a piece of cardboard, and holds it up for her to see.

"Like a baby doll," he says, illustrating the smoothness between her legs where the vagina had been. Adele sees the outline of his erection straining against his pants.

Although the chisel makes her a bit uneasy, Adele

agrees to lie back against the sofa while Leonard sets to work. She is amazed at the precision of his gestures, the careful poise of the chisel, and the deftness of his hammer coming at her again and again. But she feels nothing as he hammers away at her. Instead she closes her eyes and remembers when she first met Harry at the mall. She'd been shopping for a new pair of shoes when she was accosted by an old man jerking off while she slipped on her peds. The salesgirl had said nothing, as if she hadn't noticed the man's furious pumping, but Adele had been incensed, leaving the shoes on the floor and padding in her stocking feet to the security office located at the center of the mall. There Harry had been sitting and eating a bowl of Cheerios while reading a local newspaper. Something about the way his hat lay on his head had filled her with longing.

"I've just been accosted at the shoe store," she told him while he sopped up his cereal with a plastic spoon, "of all imaginable things."

Harry had immediately come to her rescue, running through the mall with his spoon poised like a weapon. He wrestled the old man to the ground and struck him in the groin with a pair of red heels.

"That'll teach you," he said with authority. Adele found herself gasping. It was love at first sight.

Leonard removes the drill from its case and attempts to make several holes in the center of her now missing vagina. With the sureness of a born carpenter, he tells her not to worry, that he will force it open no matter what it takes.

"If it won't let me in," he says, flexing the muscles in his upper arms and pulling at his groin, "then I'll dig my way in if I have to."

Flesh sputters out from between her legs, tiny pale flakes that float above her head and land on the black lace of the crotchless teddy. It is not painful, she is amazed to find, yet she feels a deep sense of anxiety for the woman on *The Nodderman Show* and her lost womb. When she closes her eyes, she sees the woman's tortured face, the pale mark from a runaway stroller that has marred the back of the woman's hand. Although Adele is in love with Nodderman, she is usually unmoved by the tragedy of his guests and has even found some of their suffering a kind of stimulation. But this woman is different, she thinks, has touched her in ways no other talk show panelist ever has.

"For God's sake, Leonard," she screams above the hissing of the drill, "we've just got to get it back."

Leonard nods, pulls the plastic mask over his face, and spins the drill at high speed. The flakes of skin are everywhere, and Adele can see his erection straining against his zipper. He throws down the drill and heaves himself against her, but it is as if his penis were charging against a brick wall. After several minutes he retreats with his wounded member in hand while Adele tries to guess where the missing womb might be found.

On the evening news, the anchorman reports a series of womb sightings. He speaks directly into the camera, though the cameraman is grateful for the desk that hides the reporter's erection, which would undoubtedly have a negative effect on the ratings.

"A young woman claims to have seen a womb at a shopping mall in Nashville, Tennessee, today. She reportedly found the womb on the floor of a shoe store next to a pair of size seven red heels. Authorities have examined the object and have determined that what the woman found was not a womb at all, but a rotted sponge belonging to a housewife in a local suburb."

The screen changes to a close-up of a man identified as Dr. Randolph Hand, a prominent gynecologist known for his books on painless childbirth. Behind the doctor's head is a model of a woman's reproductive system, a clay uterus with ovaries on each side the size of mothballs. The gynecologist clears his throat.

"The chances that this womb will indeed be found," he says, adjusting his glasses, "are one in five hundred thousand. It is rare enough that a womb is lost in a shopping mall, and the fact is that most people either cannot recognize a womb in all its splendor or are unwilling to take the risk of handing it over to authorities. And, of course, there is also the possibility of its being stolen by a barren or menopausal woman."

The camera cuts back to the reporter, who is straightening his tie. Behind him is a panorama of shoppers at the largest mall in the United States. Women are running frantically through the mall with their strollers; some are down on their hands and knees with armfuls of shopping bags. Everywhere there is the sound of children screaming.

After several more thwarted attempts at lovemaking, Leonard wraps his erection in an adhesive bandage. He mopes about the apartment in his briefs, switching the television on and off with the remote control. In the mornings she eats cereal and watches the cable station, tuning in for the ad for the lost womb and the hope of other sightings. Adele makes the largest omelette she has ever achieved, using an oversize pan and ten Grade A eggs.

"I think I'll go to the mall," she announces to Leonard one morning while he is swabbing his penis with cotton balls soaked in antiseptic. His tools are strewn all over the apartment and he sweats continuously. Adele cannot help but be pleased, despite herself, that he is so bent on getting back in. She puts on a pair of red heels and decides to join the search at the mall.

"And leave me here like this?" Leonard says. She can see he is weeping behind his plastic goggles, although he insists it is an occupational hazard.

She stands at the door and waves to him, the heels glinting in the overhead lights. But Leonard turns away, shielding his penis like a wounded animal. He takes out a pair of two-by-fours and begins drilling holes all over their surfaces. She stands for a moment and watches him as he stands over a two-by-four, his bandaged penis sticking straight out in front of him.

"What if it never opens again?" he calls over the high pitch of the drill.

Adele smiles briefly, and turns to walk out the door.

At the mall it takes Adele nearly an hour to find a parking space. All over the parking lot are women in black robes holding signs that say *Fruitless Wombs Unite.* Adele toots her horn at them and waves, pulling her Toyota next to the tan station wagon that she immediately recognizes as Harry's. She can feel her sealed vagina sweating in her pants as she gets out of the car. With lipstick she writes "Nodderman" on the windshield of Harry's car.

The mall is so crowded that she can scarcely make her way inside the door. There is a rally going on with signs and loudspeakers placed near the escalators. At the center of the rally is the woman from the Nodderman show, hoisted up on a stage with a sign on her breast that says simply *Rita*. Women and children run through the mall with shopping bags, knocking over plants and crawling on their hands and knees in search of the womb. On the other side of the demonstration is a group of women with baby strollers, who will participate in a relay race to show their belief in the importance of their wombs. Adele leans forward against the moving belt of the escalator, her sealed vagina bumping against the metal chinks that hold it together. *I am one of you*, she thinks, *though I never have been before*.

It is then that she sees him in the crowd, adjusting his tie and taking a long drag on a cigarette.

"Nodderman!" someone screams, and then a sea of women approach him all at once, tearing their fingernails at his white hair and shrieking with pleasure. Adele freezes as she leans against the side of the escalator trying to catch her breath, but the sight of Nodderman in all his glory is too much for her. She feels her sealed vagina pressing down between her legs.

"Oh, why me," she says as the security guards rush the mob of women, slapping at them with their hats. For a moment Nodderman stands alone, and she thinks, *I could be good to you if you'd let me*. But he does not look at her, intent instead on the wardrobe people who have come to him in droves, pulling wire brushes through the soft white hair and adjusting his glasses. She sees the woman named Rita being carried away by a security guard, her red heels dangling in the air. She strains to see if it is Harry, but the man walks away quickly, his hat pulled down over his face.

The Wall Street Journal *reports an unexplained rise in the sale of high-heeled shoes. A top financial adviser attributes the change to women's growing concern with their feet. "The days of being barefoot and pregnant," he says, "are long gone." Other experts are baffled by the sudden shift away from sneakers to heels. Perhaps women are less concerned about bunions than they once were, one says. All agree that there is one color that has outsold all the others—red.*

FIVE

At the mall Harry briefs his men about the importance of security during Nodderman's visit. It is not every day they have a man of Nodderman's stature visiting their humble mall, he reminds them. The women are bound to get carried away.

"Above all, men," Harry says, saluting them with an odd click of his heels, "don't let Nodderman out of your sight."

Harry is waiting by the escalator when the woman appears. She is more beautiful than she appeared on television. On the dim screen of his old black-and-white Sony, the paleness of her complexion had not come through. She is dressed in a red suit and matching red heels, which Harry believes have now become her trademark. For a moment he finds he cannot catch his breath, the pitiful expression on her face bringing a heat to his loins he has never before experienced.

"*I could be good to you,*" he says under his breath, "*if only you'd let me.*"

She turns toward him, and for a moment he thinks she sees him, his heart racing in his chest. He can feel the polyester of his pants stretched at the groin, the zipper teeth poking his flesh. His hat weighs heavily on his head, and he feels his throat becoming parched. If only he had some cereal, he thinks, he might have the nerve to talk to her.

"Nodderman!" he hears a woman scream, and then they are on the celebrity all at once. The women seem to come from out of nowhere, flailing red heels and matching handbags, their manicured hands reaching for handfuls of Nodderman's hair. Harry runs toward the woman with the lost womb, pounding the other women with the back of his hat. He can see the frightened look on her face, her hands twisted with worry. The ad flashes in his head, the sound of his own voice saying the words over and over, *never been pregnant, never been pregnant.*

"Give her some air," he tries to scream, but his voice comes out in only a whisper. One of the women grabs his hat and slaps him across the face with it.

"She's more than just a womb," the woman says, her eyes narrowed in disgust. "You men had better think about that."

The woman throws the hat on the floor, and kicks it away with her high-heeled red shoe. He can see Rita being carried away by one of his men, her red heels moving in small kicking gestures, like swimming. Again and again women stomp over his hat in their fury to get to Nodderman. When Harry finally gets down on his hands and knees to pick it up, he can see that the shine on the crown is gone, the once stiff brim is now wilted and crumpled. He takes the hat in his hands and sits on the floor of the mall, listening to the women screaming.

"Hey, Harry," he hears a woman say, "looks like you've lost your hat."

He turns around to see who's speaking to him, the tarnished hat lying heavily in his hands. He sees Adele in the distance, riding up the escalator and waving to him. Not a friendly sort of wave, he later thinks, but a wave that signals the end of something, a kind of dismissal. Even when she is out of sight he can still hear her laughing at him, high-pitched and girlish. On his way back to the security booth he realizes that he no longer has an erection.

SIX

L ife after *The Nodderman Show*, Rita muses one afternoon, has never been quite the same. Since her appearance she has been bombarded by letters from all types of people—sympathetic women who have spent years in fertility treatments, prepubescent girls who are at once terrified and exuberant about their ability to procreate, menopausal women who live in mourning for their drying wombs. Rita spends her afternoons watching *The Nodderman Show* and opening her mail. George carries the mail in for her in sacks, drops them on the living-room floor, and keeps one hand over his wilted penis at all times.

"Another batch has come for you," George says, leaving the letters by her feet, "while I struggle to keep control of my manhood."

She gives George a sympathetic nod and turns to her mail. The television stays on at all times, since she is never quite sure when there will be another news flash reporting a sighting of her womb or a promo for an upcoming *Nodderman* segment. She knows that all of this has taken its toll on George and that he longs for the days when she was still full of life, her womb intact, when she spent her days shopping for the perfect outfit and matching shoes. How on good shopping days she would come home and they would make love with abandon on the floor, her shopping bags strewn around them. But that Rita is gone, she thinks, and in her place has come the spokeswoman for her generation. It is, she thinks, watching George massage his limp penis, an odd place to find herself.

> *Dear Rita,*
>
> *I watched you today on* Nodderman *and my heart just went out. There you were in your high-*

heeled red shoes without a womb and here I am with
three screaming brats and a husband out of work. I
am willing to give you my oldest son, Francis, if your
womb does not turn up soon. He is twelve and has a
keen mind. I believe he'd make the adjustment.

> Yours,
> A Nodderman Fan

Rita wipes the tears away with the back of her
hand. She kicks off her heels and settles into the sofa.
Out of the corner of her eye she sees one of George's
black-and-white studies of the degeneration of his
penis, the once-full member now dwindled down to the
shadowing of a charcoal pencil.

Dear R,

> *So you live without a womb? Join the club.*
> > Signed,
> > Mrs. Menopause

She tears open another letter from a woman who
has left a lipstick blot where the return address belongs.

Dear Woman on The Nodderman Show,

   The malls are never safe. I watched you on
Nodderman *and had a good cry. I have been childless for seven years and have tried every treatment
possible. If you locate your womb sometime soon,
may I borrow it? Address enclosed. I'll pray for you.*
                        Sincerely,
                        A Fellow Womb Watcher

It is in her best interest, the Fruitless Wombs have ad-
vised her, to enclose a simple reply to every letter she
receives. To save time she has devised a note that serves
for nearly all occasions, and George has run the copies
off in a gesture of support. There is so little left that he
can do as a husband, he tells her, that some time at the
Xerox machine will do him good. She stuffs the en-
velopes with copies of the note and encloses ads for her
lost womb on colorful pink paper.

   Dear Sympathizer,

   *Thank you for your kind words. I am counting
on people like yourself to keep your eyes and ears*

open. Without you, my womb is surely lost.
Love and kisses,
Rita

She is opening the last envelope of the day when the commercial for Cheerios comes on. In the past she had never been a cereal lover, but since the promotional outing at the mall she finds she cannot get enough of it. All day long she eats bowl after bowl, the cool white milk doing its best to soothe the emptiness her missing womb has left.

"George," she calls, hastily opening the letter while the young girl on the screen delivers spoonful after spoonful of the milk into her mouth, "fix me another bowl."

She holds the letter up and strains to read the careful print, the light from the Cheerios commercial distracting her. "Dear Miss R," it says in block letters, "I could be good to you if you'd let me."

When George returns with the cereal, Rita finds she cannot stop weeping.

———

That night Nodderman calls while Rita is eating another bowl of Cheerios. George turns his head toward the phone as if to acknowledge that it no longer rings for him, that her missing womb has rendered him unmanly in the eyes of the public. No one calls to offer him sympathy, he tells her, even though his erections are a thing of the past.

"You may have lost your womb," he says, his hand cupped over his crotch in a show of protection, "but I seem to have lost my will to live."

Rita offers him the rest of her cereal as she rushes toward the phone, but it is clear that the cereal is not what he wants.

"Hello?" she says, her mouth full of milk, but already she knows that it's him. She can hear him breathing, slowly and carefully, like a talk show host.

"Are you there, caller?" he says into the phone, then giggles uncontrollably.

She opens the *TV Guide* to a photo of herself and Nodderman under the Nielsen ratings. Nodderman's ratings have gone through the roof, the article says, because of her horrifying account. She peers at her photograph, the outline of her red heels, the look of anguish on her face that has left permanent lines under her eyes and mouth. *Is that what losing my womb has done to me?* she thinks, while Nodderman's breath hisses in her ear.

"You've got to do another appearance," he says, his voice full of concern. "These women are out for blood."

He pauses for a moment, as if realizing the meaning behind his words, the image of menstrual flow the expression evokes. She twirls her spoon around in the cereal and thinks about the unsigned note and the careful handwriting. How a man could be good to her, she thought, if only he would try.

"I'd do anything to get my womb back," she tells him, with a sharpness she hadn't intended. "My life is no longer my own."

As she lets the phone hang on her shoulder, the television screen turns to static. Through the heavy blurring on the screen she can make out the shine of Nodderman's hair, standing out from the fog of the television like a beacon. How little comfort there is in her life now, she thinks, listening to the dial tone and watching Nodderman's hair flash at her over the haze of her television set.

George comes to her one night while she is trying to sleep on the sofa. The television set is on, casting an eerie light over her body in the dark. In one hand she holds the letter addressed to Miss R; in the other she clasps the week's edition of *TV Guide.* She blinks to focus, sees George kneeling by her feet, his hands slipping off the red heels.

"George," she cries, muffling her sobs in the back of her hand, "can't you see they're all I've got left?"

But before she can stop him he is all over her bare feet, rubbing his wilted penis over her pale white toes. She leans her head back in the sofa and tries to twist her feet away, but he grips her ankles, hard like a vise. After a few minutes she hears him groan, low in his throat, beads of sweat raining over her feet. He lays his head against her bare feet in shame, his pubic hairs nestled around his dysfunctional penis.

"Look at what you've driven me to," he says, pointing to the puddle of sperm around the heels of her shoes. He gets up without looking at her, as if her feet no longer mean anything to him, as if without her womb she has ceased to be the person he once knew and has turned into the sort of woman who shields even her feet from his desires.

"Oh, George, what have you done?" she says, biting the inside of her bottom lip. For the first time in weeks she feels the pain of emptiness renewed in her middle, sharp like the very first day when she lost her womb in the mall. She can hear George in the kitchen slobbering over a bowl of cereal and scratching out drawings of his erections. Only Nodderman, she thinks, picking up her violated shoes, has any hope of saving us now.

SEVEN

Rod Nodderman is alone in his bedroom when he gets a phone call from his producer. Rod is watching the taped broadcast of the woman who lost her womb in a shopping mall, a curiosity, Rod believes, which has never been seen before on national television. He freeze-frames the remote control on a close-up of him sitting at the woman's feet, her red heels dangling in the background behind his head. It is a shot for which the cameraman might win an award.

"Hello?" he says into the phone, watching the lines from the VCR create patterns on the outline of his shiny white hair. He admits to seeing a yellowish tint along the ends of the hair and thinks he might have to quit smoking to bring back its shine.

The producer is speaking so rapidly that Rod can barely make out what he's saying. Something about the whole world closing up shop, a woman's vagina sealing itself shut during his broadcast. Rod is miffed that the producer has interrupted his private viewing time—time which is only afforded him at night, after removing the make-up and applying polish to the fine white hair—and is only half-interested in the producer's speech.

"Rod," the producer says in his ear, low and full of authority, "we're talking epidemic proportions."

Nodderman releases the freeze-frame button and watches the audience on the screen pounding their breasts in empathy for the wombless woman's plight. These are words he has prayed for, he thinks, but has never consciously thought it, even during private screenings. Epidemic (or is it epic?) proportions; an exclusive broadcast. He can feel the tightening in his groin there in the dark with his own face bewitching him on the screen.

"My God, Bob," he says, putting on his eyeglasses to get a better view of his image on the screen, "book her on the show."

He hangs up the phone, acutely aware that the producer has not had the chance to tell the whole story, to explain the who's and wherefore's of the woman whose vagina has closed up shop. But it is the not knowing that intrigues him, the air of mystery he brings to his audience. *Never get the whole story,* is what he always tells insiders. No audience is interested in facts.

EIGHT

After several thwarted attempts at drilling through Adele's vagina, Leonard turns on the television. Adele lies with her legs spread on the sofa, bits of her flesh lying in piles on the floor like ashes. They watch the local news, eating peanuts and not speaking. *What is there to say,* Adele thinks to herself, *after you've lost your womanhood?*

The reporter is interviewing a private detective who is reported to be an expert in the location of missing body parts. Once he found a man's finger on a neighborhood lawn after the victim lost it in a bizarre mowing accident, on another occasion he came upon the remains of a set of teeth sent flying on a roller-coaster ride.

"My advice to this woman is not to give up hope," the man says, looking straight into the camera. "There are people out there who care."

Adele looks over at Leonard, who is sitting cross-legged on the sofa and chewing at his cuticles. He turns to her and holds up his dented hammer, with a look in his eyes that Adele thinks could only be called heart-broken. He tosses the hammer on the floor and holds both hands over his wounded penis, his shoulders shaking as he weeps and weeps.

Adele pats his shoulders and looks down at her now sexless anatomy. She thinks about all the men who have been inside her—an actor named Bob, who liked to braid her hair and sing off-color show tunes, Harry and his mall security hat, Leonard and their *Nodderman* marathons. Did she ever invite them in, she wonders, or did they simply claim her body as their rightful place? It's not that she doesn't like sex, she thinks, but seeing that woman on television who had lost her womb among thousands of shoppers has made her think about the preservation of her own body. She cannot stop thinking about the sheer pity she'd seen in Nodderman's eyes, a man whom she considers to be not easily moved, and the pull of sympathy she herself had felt. She'd seen those women parading through the mall with their strollers and heavy diaper bags; she'd had sex in the afternoons while other women were nursing and watching soap operas. All those women out there with children and vaginas had something on her, she thought, something she wanted and yet was terrified of getting.

"I've got to call Nodderman," she tells Leonard, running a hand through his hair. "It's our only hope."

She goes to the phone and dials Nodderman's toll-free number. She can feel the blood pumping through her chest and flushing her face as she listens to the ringing on the other end. Will he answer? Will she at last hear his voice? But instead she gets a screener from the network who asks Adele to recite her claim in less than three hundred words.

"Pretend you're in school," the screener says. "Nodderman's always been a sucker for essays."

She has to hold her hand over the receiver to muffle the sound of Leonard's weeping.

"I can do better than that," she says, her voice barely above a whisper. "My vagina has closed up shop."

She can hear the woman gasp on the other end of the phone, the sounds of a keyboard clicking to record her statement. Across the room Leonard picks up his hammer and begins pounding at his bloodied crotch. Adele can hear the screener catching her breath on the other end of the receiver, as if she, too, is close to tears.

"My God," the screener says, "women today are falling apart before our very eyes."

She thanks Adele for calling, but says that ultimately all decisions for broadcast are subject to Nodderman's discretion. He is a stickler for detail, she says, and they can never be sure what kind of plight will delight him on any given day.

"He's preoccupied with wombs at the moment," she says. "Maybe if you wrote him an essay he'd give it more serious consideration."

Adele hangs up the phone and looks over at Leonard. He is lying on the floor in a ball, both of his hands over his wounded penis. The hammer lies at his feet, blood speckled over the wood floor. Adele tries not to listen, but the high-pitched whimpers fill the apartment.

Dear Rod,

 For years I have been dreaming of writing you a letter.

 How odd the circumstances are. I am a woman profoundly affected by your show—so much so, in fact, that my vagina sealed itself up during your show about the wombless woman. I understand that you are preoccupied with wombs now and that vaginas are another thing entirely, but I believe that my sympathy for that poor wombless woman has left me afflicted. You are the man who can open me up again.

 Enclosed is the essay the screener suggested I write for you. I know that it is not quite 300 words, but please understand it is a difficult topic to write about. Please save me.

 Yours forever,
 Adele

MY VAGINA HAS CLOSED UP SHOP
AN ESSAY BY ADELE

for Rod

My vagina closed up one day while I was having sex while watching *The Nodderman Show.* It was on the day the guest was a woman named Rita who lost her uterus at the mall. I go to that mall; I once dated the head of security. Seeing her face there on that show made me think about all the possibilities my life once had and the fact that the only man I have wanted inside me (though there have been many) is the king of talk shows, Mr. Rod Nodderman. So that day, as if my body was finally doing the work my mind could not do, my vagina shut up right then and there right before Nodderman went to commercial.

Later that day Adele mails the letter. She spends the afternoon in front of the television set, waiting for news of further womb sightings and for Nodderman to call her back. She is so distracted by her own plight that she does not notice Leonard, who is drilling holes in apples and trying to shove his penis inside. Only when the apple splits in half and lands on the sofa does she think about what the men in the world will do without her and Rita to push around.

NEWS FLASH:

WOMB SIGHTED AT LOCAL BASEBALL FIELD
BATTER CONFUSES UTERUS FOR BALL
Associated Press, Lynchfield, Florida.

A local softball league reported seeing a womb during the area playoffs. Calvin Wood, pitcher for the local Kings, claimed he was tossed a large pink object that had been mistaken for the team's softball.

"The batter was on second, rounding the corner to third, when Chuck [first baseman] threw it to me," Wood said in an exclusive interview. "It landed right in my glove, like it had been there all its life. I went to throw it to Irv, the third baseman, when I noticed it was pink. That's when I realized we were playing with someone's womb."

Authorities later claimed that the object was not a womb at all, but a large water balloon a man had thrown in as a prank. When Rod Nodderman, the man who broke the story about the now famous missing womb, was asked to comment, he had only this to say: "A softball field is no place for any woman's womb, no matter what the circumstances."

NINE

When the size seven red heels are out of stock, it is Marty's job to take care of the reordering. He cannot stock them fast enough, it seems to him, no matter how hard he tries. Every day he makes several hundred trips to the stockroom and back out to the sales floor, where he is asked time and again whether or not he has a pair of shoes "just like that woman on television who lost her womb, size seven if you have it." Even the largest women insist on squeezing their mammoth feet into the size sevens, and he is left to shove them in with shoehorns or paste the torn seams together with masking tape. The look on the women's faces, however, is worth his minimum wage. Even the dullest woman seems to brighten with a pair of red heels on her feet. As a result he is never without an erection.

This fact is the aspect of his work his girlfriend Sarah most enjoys in the beginning, but tires of rather quickly. She refuses to wear the red heels, no matter how many pairs he brings home for her. They lie in the corner of the apartment still in their boxes, the white tissue paper fluffing out from the tops. In the half-light of the early evening, Marty thinks the shoes look like virgins, although he doesn't dare tell this to Sarah.

In the weeks since the woman with the lost womb first appeared on *The Nodderman Show*, Marty has noticed how little his life has remained stable. Sarah has taken to wearing long black robes and open-toed sandals and quoting statutes from a group of women called the Fruitless Wombs. While he is selling a record number of high-heeled red shoes, she writes hundreds of letters a day to *The Nodderman Show* and to local officials. At night when he presses his erection against the smoothness of her thigh, she switches on a taped broadcast of *The Nodderman Show* and pulls the covers tightly around her.

"This is what you men have to be sorry for," she says, biting her lower lip, although Marty does not feel any sense of guilt, no matter how hard he tries.

Perhaps it is the trouble with Sarah, he thinks, that has sent him leering at the feet of women at the shoe store. He is careful to keep a lookout for Harry, head of mall security, who is said to have no mercy on men with a penchant for women's feet. Twice he has seen Harry beat old men with the back of his security hat for jerking off outside the shoe store. Although Marty has never spoken directly to Harry, only nodded at him from inside the store window, he is sure that he and Harry are men cut from the same cloth.

Or perhaps it is the constant bombardment of wombs by the media that has driven him to this insatiable lust. Every night there is another sighting reported in the area, another diagram of a woman's insides blown up for closer inspection. A man can't drive his car home from work these days, he thinks, without being afraid of running over someone's womb on the highway. Life has taken unexpected turns.

He is sizing the feet of an eighty-year-old woman when he sees her through the glass. She is leaning forward, wearing tight blue jeans and high red heels, though he can see these were bought at another store. The old woman is pointing at the last size seven he has, bulging her eyes and taking thick gasps of air.

"Young man," she says, wiggling her varicose-veined feet under his nose, "you know the desire never leaves you, not even at my age."

He nods to the old woman and takes her wrinkled foot in his hands. The foot curls itself into a ball; he has to press the palm of his hand into her arch to make the shoe fit. All the while the woman in the tight jeans is looking at him, leaning forward from the waist, as if trying to show him something with her body. He lets his eyes fall along her waist and crotch, where he is amazed to find none of the wrinkles or folds that are normally found in women. Her jeans are seamless, he notices with wonder, her legs coming together without any disturbances. Just like a doll.

The old woman stands up and totters over to the mirror. With both hands she hoists up her knee-highs. She turns her ankles from left to right. The woman at the window gives her a thumbs-up; the old woman beams, the wrinkles on her face seeming to soften under her smile.

"If the shoe fits," the woman at the window calls to her.

Afterward Marty has to hide in the stockroom to catch his breath. When he closes his eyes he can still see the perfection of her jeans. Sweat drips from his face in thick globs. The smell of feet is everywhere. Never before, he thinks, has his heart pounded so heavily. The sight of a woman in creaseless jeans is too good to bear.

He expects the feeling to dissipate after a few days, but it continues just as strongly. At night when he wakes in a sweat, he tells Sarah that the pressures of shoe sales in the wake of the fury over red heels has left him spinning. She smiles triumphantly and says that it is just the beginning of the suffering men have to endure, that a world without wombs is a hell on earth, even for men.

"Don't even think about it," she says, slapping his erection with the back of her hand.

He bites back the tears, but later thinks it is not the pain of the slap that hurt him, but the woman in the mall looming over him in her high heels and smooth body.

At work he makes excuses for his lateness and is not able to keep up with the demands of stocking the size seven red heels. The customers berate him for being distracted, tell him it's his duty to get them the heels because a womb was lost right in that very mall.

"You owe it to us," they say, shaking their fists. "Our feet are all we have left to go on."

On his breaks he sneaks over to the mall security booth, where he watches Harry eat cereal and write letters in a careful loopy script. Marty leans against a plastic palm tree, pretending to watch the women who crawl on their hands and knees in their refusal to give up the search for the missing womb. But Harry doesn't seem to notice; he tunes in the cable station on his portable television and writes letters with the same phrasing over and over.

Dear Miss R,
I could be good to you if only you'd let me.
I could be good. If you'd let me.
If you'd let me, I'd be good.

> *Love,*
> *Harry*

What Marty is after from Harry is not clear to him at first, but instinctively he feels that Harry has something to teach him about women. He has seen the respect Harry elicits in other men, the way Harry handled himself on the day of the Nodderman appearance, the way Harry lingers outside the shoe store in the minutes before the mall closes for the night. If only he could get a look inside Harry's desk, a glimpse into his life, Marty thinks, then maybe he'd have the courage to find the woman of his dreams who stood outside the shoe store.

He finds Sarah waiting at the door of their apartment with all of her clothes tied neatly in plastic bags. When he asks where she is going, she will only say that there are women in the world who need her and that this is the beginning of a plague upon men.

"You men will have to pay the price for a world without wombs," she says, clicking her heels at the door. "No amount of red shoes can save you."

Later he thinks of the many things he might have said to her—that their months together had meant something to him (though he isn't quite sure what), that her letters to Rod Nodderman had touched him, that he was glad they'd lived through the apocalypse of the missing womb together, that he was glad to have had her to share it with. These are the things he has been told women like to hear; these are the things he has been taught to say. But she is right, he thinks, kneeling down at the doorstep and fingering a torn letter addressed to Nodderman. In a world without wombs, these things are no longer enough.

TEN

L ucy has hated the gynecologist ever since she can remember and is even more frightened now with all of the media hype about missing wombs. For years she has told herself that periodic gynecological exams are part of the liberated woman's way of life, but lately she has found that she has difficulty swallowing these ideals.

"Even having pap smears faithfully," she says to herself out loud, "cannot guarantee our safety anymore. We may as well throw caution to the wind, let our bodies rot."

Lately she has found herself believing this more

and more. The body she once prided herself in is beginning to resist the strenuous aerobics, and her muscle relaxants no longer have the same kick they once did. No longer does she feel the same joy at having the sweat run down her spandex tights or the same elation at downing a handful of Motrin after a hard day at the gym. More and more frequently she has found herself walking through shopping malls with a lump in her throat while other women push baby strollers and buy red high heels. In the afternoons she has started to call in sick to her job as a bank teller so that she won't miss *The Nodderman Show.* And when she walks her dog at night she finds herself following the dog close behind, going over on her hands and knees the areas where the dog has sniffed.

Lucy has maintained a variety of sexual partners to distract her from the melancholia she has been feeling since the womb was first reported missing. First there was Ken, the manager of a local fast-food restaurant, and then a string of bank customers who were frequent depositors. She would cling to their backs and recite their account numbers over and over in her mind to ward off the image of a womb lying frozen on her bathroom rug. Even with her legs spread wide and her fingernails embedded in their backs, she felt as if she were floating over the bed, as if her body were somehow suspended and not really a part of the sex act. She would close her eyes and try to force herself to wallow in the pleasure, to glory in the sensations that she'd heard other women boast about on talk shows.

"Scream," she would tell herself, like a director of a film, "as if you really mean it."

It was like watching herself in a home movie. She could see herself there writhing on the bed, hear the sounds coming out of her scratchy throat, but the feelings would not come. No matter how hard she tried, she was aware of herself straining to feel, of her yearning for passion. While the men thrusted and perspired on her bed, she would close her eyes and think of her womb being jostled inside her. How little it would take to make it fall out.

For a time the sex served as a diversion, but now she finds her only solace comes from watching *The Nodderman Show* in the afternoons while stroking her dog's back. The dog moans softly over the hum of her television — a symbol, she thinks, of her profound sadness.

The gynecologist's office is packed when she arrives. There are signs on the walls about how to keep your womb in place, how to keep your vagina open and healthy.

Never sit on public toilets, one sign says. Keep your legs crossed whenever possible. Give birth only when necessary. And the largest sign, in huge block letters: TUNE IN TO THE NODDERMAN SHOW.

She jots down some of these directions, takes a seat next to a potted plant, and listens to the furious whispers of the other women. *You can't be sure of anything,* they say, clasping their hands over their stomachs. *Not even liberated women are safe anymore.*

Lucy thumbs through one of the women's fitness magazines and pretends not to listen, but she cannot keep her mind on her reading. She hears one woman talking about an article she read in the morning paper. It seems, says the woman, that the plague on women has spread down to their vaginas. A woman has come forward whose vagina sealed itself shut during *The Nodderman Show.*

"If they can't get us in the womb," the woman says,

narrowing her eyes, "then they get us where we live."

Lucy feels a blush rising in her cheeks. She thinks about what that woman must have felt like to find herself sealed shut in such a way. Perhaps it is not unlike that feeling of starring in a home movie that you have no real part in. As if the cameras are rolling but no action is taking place. Lucy knows all too well what that is like. Even the dog scratching at the door at night and moaning does not reach her the way it once did. She looks down at her hands and thinks of the turn her life has taken, how she has been reduced to the solace of talk shows rather than real life, to thinking of Rod Nodderman as a surrogate lover. Perhaps with him it would be different, perhaps she'd be able to feel again. But she doubts that would be the case. Even with Nodderman, she thinks with a lump in her throat, the sex would no longer be as thrilling as walking her dog in the moonlight.

When the receptionist finally calls her name, Lucy is close to tears. She staggers into the examination room weeping as she slips into the paper gown and slides her feet into the stirrups. The gynecologist comes in, turns to her and raises an eyebrow, adjusts the sheet on her legs, and moves his face closer.

"Don't worry," he says, patting her leg. "Yours is still open."

She tries to explain that it is not her vagina she's concerned about but her life, the lives of all those women out there who are racing through the malls and sitting glued to *The Nodderman Show*. That she doesn't even know the circumstances of the woman with the sealed vagina, or the one who lost her womb, for that matter. What does she know about their lives? But all she can do is weep and talk about Rod Nodderman, about how she dreams at night of a man with white hair who talks to her in a soft voice and strokes the head of her dog.

"I just want a love life," she sobs, but the doctor has turned his back to her. He is sitting at his desk with a portable television, fiddling with the antenna to fine-tune the picture. It is *The Nodderman Show*, broadcasting live from the local shopping mall. An announcer's voice can be heard during the strains of the theme song, his voice low and packed with meaning. Lucy sits up in her paper gown, slides down the metal table to be closer to the television.

"An exclusive interview with a woman who claims her vagina sealed itself up during a broadcast of this show. It is television history in the making."

The gynecologist writes notes on Lucy's chart. He does not look at her, just scribbles a birth control prescription and tosses it over his shoulder at her. What good is birth control, Lucy feels like saying, if women no longer have the wombs or the inclination for sex?

"Refill it in six months," the doctor says. It is clear he wants to be left alone.

Lucy gathers up her paper gown and sniffles, edging closer to the doctor to watch the television over his shoulder. She does not see the blood at first, running down her leg and leaving a puddle around her feet. All she can do is watch Adele, the woman on the screen in a pair of creaseless white jeans and red heels. Adele and Rita are holding hands, Adele's fingers delicately covering the stroller mark across Rita's hand, a gesture of such comfort and protection that Lucy feels a gushing between her legs. The anguish in their faces makes Lucy press at her own stomach in sympathy. The blood spews forward in a rush.

"My God," the doctor says, getting down on his knees and mopping at the blood with a handkerchief, "it's an exclusive."

He is dialing *The Nodderman Show* before Lucy can even scream, and when she does, the women in the office come running, get down on their knees, and sob. Lucy falls to the floor and gathers the sheet between her legs. Some of the women fling themselves over her body in a gesture of overwhelming grief, but Lucy cannot feel their hands groping at her through the sheet. Even the shrill sound of their screams comes to her like a distant bell. She does not want to go on *The Nodderman Show*, she tells the women in a high-pitched voice. Her life is already too much like a television film.

"It's just too close to the real me," she says, and runs from the office. She leaves a trail of blood like an insect, the doctor says later, a female leaving its scent. All the way through the streets the blood seeps through her and forms a trail leading to her apartment. Everywhere there is the sound of dogs howling with sorrow. Perhaps this is what it feels like to be in heat, she thinks, remembering the stains that her dog leaves on the carpet periodically, the way the dog laps at itself during those times, as if ashamed. She runs up the steps to her apartment, the blood trailing behind her. How sad, she thinks, her heart aching at the thought of her dog trying to hide the telltale signs of her desire, to have everyone know what is happening to your body. To have everyone know how badly you are wanting.

At home Lucy shoves a roll of toilet paper between her legs and barricades her door. The dog is waiting for her, wagging its tail and trying to lap up the trail of blood behind Lucy as best it can. Lucy sits on the floor and wraps her arms around the dog, her chest heaving with the constant sobs.

"I'll never doubt you again," she says, kissing the dog on the nose, the wetness stinging her lips.

Already she can hear the reporters setting up their cameras and doing sound checks. Her apartment was easy to find, she realizes, since the trail of blood led right to her door. She can hear the cameras clicking outside in the hall as they take flash pictures of the blood trail. Soon everyone at the bank will know, she thinks, downing a handful of birth control pills. She wonders if the men she has slept with will close their accounts. She imagines herself on the stage of *The Nodderman Show*, the blood seeping into the audience.

"I only wanted some company," she would say, as she told the audience of all the one-night stands with the men from the bank, and her body's inability to feel.

The dog whimpers softly and lays its head in Lucy's lap. She can hear the slamming of apartment doors, the frantic whispers of her neighbors, the cries for maintenance to shampoo the hall rug. She locks the deadbolt and tries to block out the noise, but she can feel people looking at her, even through the door, their eyes burning at the sight of her blood. It is just like being on television, she thinks, only the cameras have not yet found their way inside.

She stands at the door and pleads with the cameramen to leave her in peace. She just wants to be alone with her dog, she says, to mourn the loss of her anonymity.

"There's nothing Nodderman can do for us now," she sobs against the door. "All the years without feeling have forced my body to spring a leak."

After a time the cameramen murmur that they will leave her alone for the time being, but that they will be back for an exclusive broadcast. As a woman, they say, she owes the American people that much.

When she thinks it is safe, she gets up from the floor and waddles through the apartment with her bathroom rug between her legs. If she can just contain the blood in some way, she thinks, perhaps this will end, like a bad dream. She cannot stop herself, though, from turning on the television and watching *The Nodderman Show* with the blood seeping between her legs. She moves from room to room, mopping up her trail with the rug and some old cloth towels, but the blood keeps coming. The dog sniffs at the blood and howls. Nodderman smiles at the camera, his white hair shining under the camera lights.

"There you have it, folks," he says with a glint in his eye. "This is what's happened to the women of today."

The reporters bang on the door, and Lucy can hear the hissing sounds of a hound sniffing at her welcome mat. Her dog curls itself at her feet and whimpers, the blood soaking through the paper towels and onto her polished floor. The woman on the television stands to a thunder of applause, the smoothness of her crotch caught in a wide-angle shot. There must be some way to stop the blood, Lucy thinks, and stuffs a small pillow inside herself. But in a few minutes the bleeding soaks through, and she is left standing there in a pool of redness while Nodderman leads the audience in a rousing chorus of an old Helen Reddy song. Despite herself, Lucy finds she cannot stop humming along.

Late that night Lucy calls all the men she has slept with from the bank and leaves messages on their answering machines. Her dog stands on its hind legs with its front paws in the air. Lucy feels a lump in her throat but forces herself to speak each time.

"Ron," she says, and then replaces the name each time with the next one—Charles, Tom, Lou, Warren—"each time we made love it was like the movie of my life. Perhaps one of these days I'll see you on television."

She waits by the telephone for one of the men to call her back, but she is not really surprised when the phone does not ring. She sleeps on the sofa with the dog at her feet, a pile of old newspapers stuffed between her legs. During the night the blood soaks through the newspapers and leaves words all over her couch, the thick newsprint bleeding down into the carpet. There on the pale carpet within the circle of blood is a picture of Rod Nodderman waving to reporters. Even through the darkness of the newsprint and the redness of the blood, she cannot help noticing how well his white hair shines.

The bleeding goes on and on. Lucy is unable to work and does not leave her apartment for any reason. After a few days she does not bother to make excuses for her absence at the bank. Anyone walking down the street is aware of the trail she has left. Several policeman have even been called to stand guard at the curb to keep the trail of blood from being washed away by the scuffing of people's feet.

"This is one incident," a policeman says, "that we will not allow to be swept away."

After a few days Lucy begins to feel accustomed to the few rooms in which she lives, to only catching glimpses of the outside world through her window or on the television set. She develops a routine of eating food from cans and watching television day and night, singing to her dog when the mood strikes. The reporters have remained camped outside her door, passing notes to her under the carpet.

We just want a few shots of you bleeding, the notes say, *or a couple of quotes about menstruation. Why won't you give us that much?*

But she does not answer the notes, tries to drown out the sounds of the reporters by turning the volume on *The Nodderman Show* up high. Without her dog and the sound of Nodderman's voice, she thinks, she would surely lose her mind.

One of her neighbors brings her a tray of Saltines and a box of sanitary napkins. She slides each napkin and each carefully buttered Saltine under the door.

"Oh, Lucy," the neighbor says in a plaintive voice, "can't you see how much Nodderman needs you?"

But she doesn't answer. Instead she feeds the Saltines to her dog, one by one. The dog wags its tail and licks the butter from her fingertips. Together they swallow the last of her birth control pills and stretch out on the floor. The blood drips from her legs and around the outline of her body in a kind of moat. Since the dog has been in heat, Lucy feels that she can understand the depth of her suffering. They howl into the night, waking the neighbors with their racket. The dog laps up the blood with frantic swipes of its tongue, its nipples and abdomen swollen with sympathy. A baby is screaming down the hall, the harsh gulps of air and incessant sound reverberating through the halls. Lucy imagines the baby, red-faced and screaming, and thinks about what she might do to comfort it if it were hers. She tries to hum a lullaby in her throat but all that comes out is a breathy sound, like moaning. Who is she fooling, after all. No matter what she does, she cannot even comfort her own whimpering dog.

Sometime before dawn the telephone rings. The apartment is quiet; the dog lies within the circle of Lucy's blood on the carpet. Perhaps the reporters have gone home for a while, she thinks, have given her a chance to bleed in peace. She pads over to the telephone and lifts the receiver. Which one is it, she wonders, running through the list of men she has slept with the past several months. She holds the receiver to her chest for a moment, hoping that whoever it is will hear the pounding of her heart through the receiver.

"Hello?" she says finally, the word sticking in her throat, her mouth dry and pasty.

There is a long silence, and then the sound of a voice she has never heard before.

"I know what it's like to bleed," the man says, and then there is the muffled sound of sobs, the click as he hangs up before she can answer.

For a long time she lies there on the couch with her feet resting on her dog's back. The blood runs down her legs and over her feet, the redness caked between her toes. She nudges the dog with her foot, but the dog is sleeping so soundly that it does not move. Lucy tries to fall back to sleep, but the voice replays itself again and again in her head. Whoever that was, she thinks, she will not likely meet him. No man can truly know what it feels like to bleed.

ELEVEN

Rita and Rod Nodderman are eating scrambled eggs in the Green Room, waiting for Adele. Nodderman is hardly eating his eggs, Rita notices; he can barely contain his excitement. But Rita is famished, devours her own helping and then Nodderman's with minimal gasps for air.

Nodderman paces the room, his erection pushing at the zipper of his pants. Rita can see that nothing about him has changed, that after all this time of knowing her womb is out in the world somewhere, he has for the most part remained unaffected. Even when the audience cheers his name, it is a kind of distant bell, Rita thinks, as if everything he sees and hears is filtered through water.

She was once that way herself, and she has come to recognize the signs. She remembers the days when she could walk through a mall amid the screams of toddlers and the scrape of strollers on the pavement without distraction. But now the sounds are an assault, as if the loss of her womb has stripped her of her defenses. She can scarcely watch a television commercial without feeling on the edge of tears.

And then there is George, constantly drawing shadows of his once powerful penis and dragging her mail in like a servant. Each time he stares down at her heels, she can feel the lump swelling in her throat. Recently they have started avoiding each other, eating their cereal in separate rooms and watching separate channels on television. It is, she thinks with a sigh, no way for a young couple to live, with or without a womb to hold them together.

Adele appears at the door in a pair of white jeans and tight-fitting red heels. The fork is poised outside Rita's waiting mouth, ready for another scoop of scrambled eggs, when their eyes meet. Nodderman stands in the corner of the room with his hands in his pockets as if he is searching for something that neither of them can give. Later Rita thinks that the moment occurred for her in slow motion, as if there were a cameraman inside her head freezing the moment frame by frame. The whole room seems hazy except for the blaring whiteness of Nodderman's hair and the stain of soggy eggs on the front of her white blouse. She throws her arms open and runs to Adele, the two of them weeping in each other's arms. Even Nodderman seems moved, although not nearly to tears.

"It's you," they say simultaneously. Nodderman wipes at his nose with a paper napkin.

After a minute Rita lets go of Adele and stands watching her. The depth of feeling she sees in Adele's eyes is greater than any she has ever seen in George's, Rita thinks, or in any other man's for that matter. Wordlessly they move to the table and sit. Rita holds the forkful of scrambled eggs and begins feeding Adele bits of egg from her plate.

"Somebody get Bob in here!" Nodderman screams. "This is the stuff television is made of!"

Adele eats the eggs hungrily, her eyes closed, one hand holding on to the sleeve of Rita's jacket. Rita is grateful to be feeding Adele, scrapes the eggs with her fork tenderly, lifting the fork with the greatest care. She thinks back to the days when George would eat crumbs from her hand after they'd made love and baked brownies. As he licked the crumbs from the palm of her hand, his tongue lapping, she'd never been more content. She wishes that she had a bowl of cereal to feed Adele, but Nodderman tells her there is not a drop of milk left in the studio.

"Save some of this rapport for the show," he whispers to them, and then is dragged off to make-up. Rita notices that his glasses are fogged and she thinks that perhaps seeing the two of them together may have gotten to him. But he is only one man, she realizes, and cannot speak for the masses, no matter how hard he tries. Still they are faceless, wombless, vaginaless women against the world.

When the producer comes to tell them there are only a few minutes left to air time, Adele begins to weep again. Rita wraps a protective arm around her and together they make it to the soundstage, and sit under the hot lights. The cameraman pins a microphone to each of their lapels. Rita can see he is straining not to reveal his erection. All the while Adele holds on to Rita's hand, rubs her red pump against Rita's own. Rita smiles at the camera, her heart swelling for the first time since she lost her womb in the mall. How sad it is, she thinks, that one has to sink so low before finding happiness such as this.

"And so you have it, folks," Nodderman says, pulling his microphone in close and speaking in a deep voice, "a woman so profoundly affected by my show that her sex organ sealed itself shut during a broadcast."

The audience murmurs; several of the women slide their feet against the carpet. Rita manages not to look at any of the audience members directly, casts her eyes to the back of the auditorium, where George sits with his drawing pad. She can never be sure what kind of effect her lost womb will have on people. Here with Adele shivering in the seat next to her, she realizes the true power of her own womb. Women will go to such great lengths to get it back, seal themselves shut in sympathy. It is, she thinks, a sobering fact.

Nodderman walks up to the stage and takes Adele by the hand. He motions for her to stand up and twirl around so that the audience at home can get a good view of her creaseless crotch. Rita nods to her, and Adele stands, wobbly at first, her red heels quivering under her weight.

"Think of all the women you may be saving," Nodderman says under his breath. He gives Rita a knowing look.

Adele stands on the stage, her legs slightly apart, the smoothness of her white jeans evident between her legs. "Close-up!" Nodderman screams, and with the camera frozen there, Rita finds herself gasping at the depth of Adele's suffering in her name.

The camera turns to George, who is hulking in the back of the auditorium, his hand over the front of his pants. The shame is written all over his face, the starkness of the charcoal-pencilled penis glaring out from the drawing pad like a threat.

"Let this be a lesson to you!" someone screams at George, and then the audience is on him, tearing the drawing pad out of his hands and holding the picture of his wilted erection under the camera lights. Rita tries to run to him, sees the frightened expression on his face, but Nodderman holds her back, stepping on her red heels to keep her from moving.

"Let them have him," he says, squeezing the stroller mark on her hand. He turns to the camera, smiles without revealing his teeth. "We'll be back after these words."

Before Nodderman can find them, Rita pulls Adele down the hallway and into the Green Room. "To turn on George that way," she says, "is a sign that things have gone too far. The lost womb has driven the audience into a frenzy. We've got to make a run for it," she says. "These women are out for blood." Adele just nods, hands Rita the essay she wrote to get on *The Nodderman Show.*

"It's really for you," Adele says. "Without that womb we're nothing."

They gather up their purses and head out the back door to the parking lot. Rita fumbles in her purse for her keys, smears her hands with violet lipstick. She can hear the Fruitless Wombs chanting behind them, pounding their sandals into the gravel of the parking lot. Even without her womb, she realizes, she does not want to be one of them. It is for her a rare moment of clarity, which she has had only once before, in the shoe store, just before losing her womb.

"It was like this," she tells Adele in the car. "Right there in the shoe store window I saw my womb flash before my eyes, clear and pink as I'd ever imagined it might be. Look at all these women, I said to myself, with their strollers and diaper bags. And what did I have but a pair of red heels, my favorite, size seven. I knew my life would never be the same."

Rita turns the key with a start, races the engine. Adele takes hold of her hand and before they know it they are laughing. Behind them in a cloud of dust is George, waving his drawing for her like a banner. "God save my womb," she says, squeezing Adele's hand and flooring the accelerator. In all the excitement, she later tells herself, she simply didn't realize how she'd left him behind that day. At the time she'd only wanted to get away from Nodderman.

TWELVE

NODDERMAN GUESTS
ON THE LAM

At a press conference this afternoon, Rod Nodderman read a prepared statement regarding the guests who disappeared yesterday from his weekly syndicated television show. According to audience members, the two women fled the stage after witnessing the attack on one of the women's husband during a commercial break. The woman, known all over the country as Rita, the woman who stole the hearts of thousands with the sad account of her lost womb, is said to have shook her fist behind Nodderman's back and declared him a traitor to all women. Mr. Nodderman read the following statement in response to these charges:

"These women, Adele and Rita, were brought to my attention of their own accord. It is my duty as a broadcaster and public servant to tell their tales on television. I did so to the best of my ability, only to have them walk off during a live broadcast which would undoubtedly have made television history. . . . The womb remains lost to this day, and I feel sure that if they hadn't fled, Miss Rita would have her womb safe inside her, and Miss Adele would be open once again."

Rita's husband, who would identify himself only as George, could not be reached for comment, although spectators say he was last seen in the Nodderman parking lot making charcoal drawings of his sexual organ and selling them to passersby.

THIRTEEN

Rita and Adele check into a motel room under assumed names, Harriet and Gloria. They tell the motel clerk in hushed voices that they are sisters and need a quiet retreat to get over the recent loss of their mother, Gladys. "Perhaps you read about it in the newspaper," Adele says; "she was struck in the head by a piece of rotten fruit. A freak accident." Rita nudges her with her elbow to tell her she's taking it too far. The clerk offers them a basket of fruit in sympathy.

"Here you've lost your poor mother," the clerk says, fighting back tears, "and I can think of nothing but that poor lady and her womb. I hope," the woman says, motioning to the basket, "that this won't be too great a reminder of your mother's untimely death."

Rita thanks the woman and takes Adele by the arm. They walk out to their room together, holding their breath to keep from laughing, just like schoolgirls. Inside the room they tear open the fruit basket and flop down on the twin beds, munching on the apples and kicking off their red heels.

"And to think," Adele says wistfully, "I once thought I could never live without Nodderman."

For several hours they lie across their beds without speaking. The depth of their connection, Rita thinks, goes far beyond words. She finds herself thinking of George huddled in the parking lot with his drawings, Nodderman and the fury in his eyes. The fact that she lost her womb has overshadowed her life, she realizes, and she simply needs a chance to regroup. How nice it will be to wake up without a sackful of mail and George with his dick in his hands. For the first time in months, she walks barefoot, the motel room carpet cool beneath her toes.

On the opposite side of the room, Adele continues to

think about Nodderman, no matter how hard she tries not to. When she closes her eyes she can still see the shock on his face when she and Rita fled the stage. She'd said the words mentally over and over again in the hopes that he'd read her mind, but he'd never shown her a sign. *I could be good to you*, she carves in the motel desk, *if only you'd let me.*

While Rita is sleeping she writes a note to Leonard in block letters. She does not want him to get the wrong idea, and so avoids the romance of a loopy script. She takes her time, thinking of the best way to express her feelings, but realizes finally that there is no other way to say it.

Dear Leonard,

We had some good times. Don't fool yourself into thinking we didn't. But without my vagina we have nothing left. Even you can see that. Pack up your hammers and find another vagina. Or drill your way into another woman's heart. In any case, get on with it. This vagina will no longer open for you.

Love,
Adele

She knows that Rita will disapprove of the letter, although she hasn't said so. They have developed that kind of rapport. When Adele hears the Nodderman theme song running through her head, Rita at the same moment begins to hum the song. It is the kind of empathy, Adele thinks, that only two women can have.

During the night Adele slips out the door and mails the letter outside the clerk's all-night office. Through the clerk's window she can see the television playing, a rerun of a *Nodderman* segment that aired before the womb had even been lost. She scrapes the heel of her red pump into the pavement and sighs. For good measure she removes one of her red heels and places it inside the mailbox. It hits the bottom with a heavy metal clang that reverberates through the dark lot.

FOURTEEN

L ucy wakes to find her dog lying motionless on the living room floor. At first she thinks that the dog is merely in a deep sleep, having been kept awake all night by the reporters. But when she nudges the dog's back with the ball of her bare foot, it is clear that the dog is no longer breathing.

"Oh, Sophia," she cries, shaking her fists in the air, "you were the only one who knew what it was like to bleed."

She falls down on her hands and knees, weeping. The dog is covered in Lucy's menstrual blood, its eyes and teeth caked over with redness. It seems the dog tried too hard, Lucy thinks, to lap up the evidence of Lucy's blood. Its abdomen is swollen to bursting, as if the dog's womb has taken in all of Lucy's grief. Lucy wraps the dog in newspaper and places it in front of the television set. Even dogs are no longer safe, she thinks between sobs, with that womb out there alone in the world. She wipes a blood-stained hand over the dog's head, stroking it one last time.

She thinks about the days when Sophia was a pup, how it used to dig Lucy's tampons out of the garbage as if they were some sort of prize. And the days when the dog was grown and the two of them went walking in the moonlight, all the times the dog had been in heat. Perhaps she should have allowed the dog to have a litter of pups. Both of their lives might have been different if the dog had given birth. Or it might have been more humane to have it neutered. At least then she might have saved the dog from the suffering, the agony of being unfulfilled.

Before she can think about what she is doing, she is dialing *The Nodderman Show*. When the screener asks her why she wishes to speak to Rod Nodderman personally, Lucy says in a quiet voice that Nodderman needs her as much as she needs him, that his connection with afflicted women is a two-way street.

"Tell him if he wants good television," she says, pulling the towels from between her legs and letting the blood rush forth in a torrent, "that he knows where to find me."

Nodderman is on the phone in a matter of seconds, his breath hissing through the receiver. After months of watching the show, Lucy would know the sound of his breath anywhere. For a minute he says nothing, and Lucy is left there with the receiver on her shoulder and Sophia wrapped in newspaper at her feet like an offering.

"The bleeding won't stop," she says in a whisper, "not with that womb out there in the world. Even my dog has become a casualty."

She stands weeping while Nodderman murmurs in her ear, soft words of consolation about the show's commitment to women.

"We've all been affected by this," he says after a long pause, "my show most of all."

The producer comes on then, tells her in a loud voice that she should let the cameramen in now, and to keep the dog within view.

"This is something the people will want to see," he says, and Lucy nods, hanging up the phone before he can finish with his instructions.

For a moment she stands over Sophia, the drops of her blood raining over the pages of the newspaper like tears. She tears a large piece of the newspaper for herself and sticks it between her legs. With the last bit of dignity she can muster, she opens the front door.

"Film me any way you choose," she says, as she slips into a pair of red heels, "but leave my dog in peace."

She sits on the sofa and waits for Nodderman to arrive. After all these months of watching him, she feels that she already knows him, that meeting him, in fact, will be anticlimactic. She thinks of all the deposits she has dreamed of making in Nodderman's name, of the bank customers who have come and gone to help her stave off loneliness. And how, through it all, there was always her dog running at her heels, lapping at whatever mess Lucy left behind. Only a dog, she thinks, is capable of such devotion.

The cameraman runs toward her and rubs pancake make-up all over her face, then hits her in the face with an enormous powder puff. He turns her face this way and that, looking through his camera to see which is her better side. Lucy sees herself in the reflection of his lens, her sagging shoulders and drooping lids. The glare of her red heels, she thinks, is the only thing that might save her.

"Keep the dog within arm's length," the cameraman says, "and just let the blood flow."

She nods, wipes at her eyes with a soiled handkerchief. She sits on the sofa with her red heels hanging in the air above the dog's carcass, the blood forming puddles around the dog's stiff ears. Rod Nodderman bursts into the apartment with a basket of flowers in his hand, kneels in front of her with his hands over his heart.

"Help us find those women," he says, his erection straining in his pants, "and we'll buy you a brand-new dog."

Lucy says nothing, just sniffles as the make-up man powders her nose and mouth, highlights her cheeks with rouge. They don't want her to seem as if she's lost all that blood, he tells Nodderman. They want the

American people to feel sympathy for Lucy, but not alarm. Alarm is never a good thing on television.

"You see what this womb has done to us," the make-up man says, "We've all begun to crack under the strain."

Nodderman rakes a nervous hand through his white hair.

When the camera starts rolling, Lucy hears Nodderman narrating the story of the lost womb in a low monotone. All she ever wanted was to feel things—the touch of a familiar man in her bed, the love of a good dog, the rush of excitement that other women had told her about. But now all she hears is the sound of babies screaming even when she plugs her ears.

"When did all this begin for you?" Nodderman asks, reaching out to hold her blood-splattered hand.

She takes a deep breath, then looks directly into the camera.

"When I started watching *Nodderman*," she says.

The camera pans to a shot of Lucy's dog lying dead on the living room floor. Nodderman reaches down and peels a layer of the newspaper from the dog's body. He gasps at the sight of his own face imprinted on the dog, the newsprint having bled over the dog's skin.

"Run a close-up of this," he whispers to the cameraman, and there on Lucy's television is the image of her sitting on the sofa with her red heels dangling, her dog on the floor in a puddle of bloody newsprint, forever marked by the face of Rod Nodderman. She lets out a long sigh and covers her face in her hands. Somehow she knew her life would come to this, with her face on the television screen and her heart in her throat. Even in a time of crisis like this, she can see her face on the screen lined with grief, the pools of blood near her feet, but all of it comes to her filtered through television, as if it is not really her up there at all, but some woman who is meant to bring the grief home to her, enlarged and in color on her twenty-six-inch set.

Nodderman cuts to a commercial, squeezes her hand, and pounds his fist to his chest.

"Wherever that womb is now," he says, "there is no one out there who can hide from it."

When he comes back from commercial, he tells the cameraman to begin with a clip from the womb's initial disappearance. Lucy wipes her eyes and feels the blood dripping from her as they show various scenes from past *Nodderman* shows depicting the saga of the womb. In the last shot is a huge photo of Rita on her first appearance on the show, staring out at the audience with an empty look in her eyes.

Vacant, one of the producers comments, as if there were no longer anything left inside. As if the womb had taken it all.

FIFTEEN

In the weeks following Rita's disappearance, Harry is demoted from his job as head of mall security. Too much has happened, one of the security officers tells him, to let things go along unchecked. In a matter of several weeks, there have been two break-ins at the shoe store and at least four incidents of women being accosted by masturbating old men.

"I don't know what's gotten into you, Harry," the chief mutters, "but you seem to have lost your edge."

Harry takes the news with as much dignity as he can muster. He turns in his security hat and clears his desk of all remnants of Cheerios boxes. Perhaps the job needs a younger man, he thinks, the kind of man with something at stake, a reason to risk his life for faceless shoppers. With Rita gone he can no longer pretend to be interested in the crowds at the mall, even the women with bags full of shoes. He has not had an erection in nearly a month, and admits that maybe the job needs an element of sexual tension.

On his way down the mall escalator he finds a piece of a torn letter he has written to Rita. He rubs his fingers over the careful print, thinks of her face glowing on the television, the swell of his penis as he watched her cable ad. He could have been good to her, he thinks, wiping his eyes with the back of his hand, but now she seems to be gone forever on account of a bad day on *The Nodderman Show*.

He stops outside the shoe store for a last look around. The shelves are stocked with size seven red pumps, the heels in varying widths and heights. The salesclerk, a young guy named Marty, waves to him from the sales floor.

"Hey, Harry," Marty calls as Harry turns away, "is it true you once went out with Adele?"

Harry stops by the door and waits for Marty to catch up to him. Marty is red-faced and sweating, his face flushed with excitement. Harry thinks he can see himself in Marty, the once-daring charm, the youthful vigor. How all of that has wilted under the weight of a security hat and an empty life.

"Yes," Harry says, turning to walk away.

He is almost outside when he hears Marty calling to him again, the words reverberating through the mall.

"Do you think that womb will ever turn up?"

Harry stands in the doorway, feels the breeze on his hatless head, the torn letter tucked away inside his polyester security pants.

"God knows," he says, and makes his way outside the mall.

At home Harry eats a bowl of Cheerios while watching the evening news. After three weeks, the reporter says, the women from *The Nodderman Show* have not yet turned up. In the meantime a full-blown investigation into the recent phenomena has ensued. They will surely get to the bottom of all that's happened, the reporter says—a missing womb, a sealed vagina, a bleeding woman and her dead dog. These are no ordinary occurrences.

"You can say that again," Harry says to himself. He can feel the tears welling, forces himself to swallow the cereal to keep from crying. He presses the remote to get away from the reminders of Rita, but all that comes on is the cable ad for the lost womb, the large pink letters floating across the blackness of the screen.

SIXTEEN

A young hemophiliac man is found dead in a motel room with a plastic womb tied around his neck. The motel clerk testifies that she found the man some time after midnight, shortly after the *Nodderman* exclusive taping at the bleeding woman's apartment. The man had checked in that afternoon, said he only planned to stay a few hours. The clerk says she wrote him a receipt (he paid cash) and bade him good-night.

"I remember thinking," the clerk says, "that something about the boy reminded me of blood, but at the time I could not put my finger on it."

Police found the young man after a neighbor at the motel complained of a television blasting *The Nodderman Show* after midnight. Officials say the man had no other possessions but the plastic womb and a suitcase full of women's high-heeled shoes. The motive is unknown, officials say, although there are rumors of a typewritten note found clutched in the man's right hand.

Dear Lucy, the note said. *I could have been good to you if only I'd lived.*

SEVENTEEN

It is nearly time for Marty's lunch break when the young man comes into the shoe store. Since the woman with the creaseless vagina disappeared, Marty finds lunchtime to be his only relief. He spends his lunch hour sitting outside the mall security booth where Harry once worked and eats day-old tuna-fish sandwiches. When there are no shoppers around, he tries to peer inside the security booth for a look at what was once part of Harry's world. In some small way he finds it a comfort to know that Harry was once inside the woman who so relentlessly shut herself up, that he is able to work in the same mall where the womb was reportedly lost. But these small facts do not serve to console him for very long.

The man approaches Marty with a kind of purpose in his eyes, as if he knows what he wants before he even asks for it. It has become passé, Marty thinks, to see such certainty in the wake of the fury over red shoes. For a moment he thinks about Sarah, how she too had that look, had been so focused in her pursuit of Nodderman and the lost womb. He has never experienced that intensity himself, except in his brief encounter with Adele, and even then he knew that a sealed vagina was not an easy obstacle to overcome.

"May I help you?" Marty asks the man, with his salesman smile securely in place. Luckily he is still able to play the role, although he finds himself checking his watch and counting the minutes until lunchtime. He feels in his pocket for the tuna sandwich.

The man squares his shoulders, looks Marty directly in the eye.

"I'm a hemophiliac," the man says, loudly, startling the other customers, "and I want nothing more than to buy some women's shoes."

For a minute Marty says nothing. Then he takes the man by the arm and leads him to a corner of the shoe store where he won't cause such a commotion. Have some decorum, he wants to tell the man. There are people buying shoes in this store. But he cannot bring himself to say it and instead offers the man a piece of his tuna sandwich. The man shakes his head and points to the size seven red heels.

"I'll take as many as you have," he says, and shakes Marty's hand, the tuna fish squishing between Marty's fingers.

Marty tells the man that in his experience the red heels are overrated, that the fury over the lost womb has caused women to be far too interested in a product with little lasting value. Secretly he hopes the man will change his mind, since he cannot bear to think of parting with the last dozen or so pairs he has left in the store.

"How about a nice white sandal," Marty says, holding the shoe up for the man, "or a silky black stiletto heel?"

But the man shakes his head, grabs the red heels, and shoves them at Marty.

"These are the ones I want," he says, and Marty knows from the look in his eyes that there is no talking him out of it.

In the stockroom Marty takes down all the boxes of red heels and piles them on the carpet. One last look, he tells himself, and opens each box, letting the white tissue puff out from over the top. He thinks of Adele suspended in front of the shoe store, wrapped in white tissue paper and a big red bow.

I could have been good to her, he thinks, *if only she hadn't run away.*

There are seventeen pairs left, all of them size seven. Marty carries them up front to the cash register and piles them on the counter. The man opens each box, peering inside, as if he senses Marty's unwillingness to part with them.

"If you knew what I'm going to do with them," the man says in a low voice, "you wouldn't feel half so bad."

Marty nods and rings up the order. Ordinarily it is the salesgirl's job to ring up the shoes, but this time Marty feels the need to do it himself. One by one he enters the prices, smearing the register keys with tuna fish from his fingers. The man opens his wallet and

128

counts out his bills, reaching into his pocket for the exact change.

"I hope you enjoy them," Marty says, handing the man the shoes, but once he has said it he realizes how foolish it sounds. The man turns to Marty and gives him a sad smile. He lifts one of the shoes out of its box as if to salute him.

"At this point," the man says, "enjoyment is no longer part of it."

Marty watches as the man walks away. He can see by his watch that it is lunchtime, but he no longer feels the same excitement. After the man is gone he paces the floors of the mall, staring down at the floor for signs of the lost womb. He takes in a deep breath to try to clear his head of the image of Adele in her creaseless white jeans. Every time he closes his eyes he is assaulted by the image of the deep hunger in the hemophiliac's eyes, the sharp smell of tuna fish.

That night he watches the news alone in his bedroom, waiting for signs of Adele. The reporter tries to interview Nodderman, but he declines to comment for the record. In the dim light he watches Nodderman's face on the television set and reads old letters from Sarah. Maybe if they'd had a child, he thinks, things would have been different. He feels an ache in his crotch at the thought.

At first he does not recognize the hemophiliac when a photo of him flashes across the screen. He is making himself a fresh tuna sandwich and thinks that the smell of the mayonnaise has brought back memories of the traumatic day in the shoe store. How he'd been forced to sell his last pairs of the red heels and didn't even have the desire for lunch. *Tomorrow is another day*, he tells himself, *and it won't be long before the heels are restocked*. It is, after all, his job.

He is taking his first bite when he sees the picture of a man's body being removed from a motel room. Around his neck, says the reporter, was the plastic model of a woman's uterus. "This thing has driven all of us too far," one of the onlookers says, and Marty feels the tuna fish stick in his throat.

There on the lawn of the motel are piles of women's red pumps that have been recovered from the man's motel room. Even under the harsh lights of the camera, in the humid night air, the heels still shine, Marty notices.

"He was a hemophiliac," one of the policemen says, "and had apparently watched too much *Nodderman.*"

The camera switches to a photo of Lucy, a woman who has not stopped bleeding since Adele's disappearance. Marty swallows his tuna fish as the reporter reveals a photo of the woman's dead dog lying at Nodderman's feet.

"How many pairs of shoes were there?" the reporter asks the policeman.

Marty feels his breath tighten in his throat, the mayonnaise thick on his tongue and teeth.

"Seventeen," the policeman says.

After a few minutes Marty turns off the television set. He shoves the half-eaten sandwich into the pocket of his robe and begins to weep, softly at first, and then louder and more harshly. All he can think of is Harry sitting at the mall security booth with his hat in his hands, how lucky he'd been to have Adele. How they all hoped so desperately that the womb would turn up, but that now, with every passing day, the future looked more and more bleak. The thought of going back to work and facing all those empty shelves is nearly too much for him to bear.

EIGHTEEN

During the night Rita and Adele are awakened
by the sound of sirens and the glare of red
flashing lights. They rub their eyes and sit at
the edge of their beds, their bare feet dangling over the
sides. Rita gathers the sheet around her and stares at
Adele, feels the familiar emptiness in her middle where
the womb had once been.

"The jig is up," Rita says, moving over to the window. "It looks like they've come for us."

She moves the drapes aside with her hand to see
what is happening outside. With the moonlight coming

through the window she can see the stroller mark across the length of her hand, although it has begun to fade. Adele stands beside her and places a hand on her shoulder. Rita lets out a long sigh. She thinks of George alone somewhere with only the comfort of his drawings, and the memory of her crotchless red teddy. *Maybe it is time to go back,* she thinks, although she's not sure what she'll be going back to.

Outside she sees a group of police officers standing on the motel lawn. As far as she can tell, there is no camera crew there yet, though she believes Nodderman will not be far behind. One of the policemen is standing next to a stretcher with a long black body bag and a suitcase full of red heels.

"My God, Adele," she gasps when she catches sight of the plastic object in the officer's hand, "my womb has gone and killed someone."

She runs from the window and throws herself down on the bed, hiding her face under the blankets. It is bad enough for all the world to know she lost her womb in a shopping mall, she sobs, but to have it be responsible for someone's death is more than she can bear. If only she had been more careful that day, she thinks, if only she hadn't bought the red heels, how different her life might have been.

"My womb," she says to Adele, her voice muffled under the blankets, "is now not an instrument of life, but of death."

Adele sits next to her on the bed and tugs gently at her shoulder. From under the blankets Rita hears her murmuring words of encouragement, although she cannot clearly make them out. After all that has happened, she still has Adele to lean on in moments of crisis. Nothing can compare to the depths of another woman's sympathy, she thinks, as evidenced by Adele's own sealed vagina. In a world without wombs, at least they will have each other to count on.

After a time Rita feels calm enough to raise her head from under the blankets. She finds Adele sitting and smiling at her, a sad sort of smile that speaks to her of her own longing and forgetfulness, the profound guilt of once having had a womb and losing it so carelessly in a mall. She has a responsibility, she realizes with some regret, to put an end to the suffering on her behalf.

They spend the rest of the night watching reruns of *The Nodderman Show* with the sound off. There is something about a man on television, Rita says, which still intrigues her after all of this. The shiny white hair and cool blue eyes, the way the lenses of his glasses reflect the camera lights. There was a moment on stage, she tells Adele, when she saw her own reflection in the lenses of Nodderman's glasses, the emptiness of her stare up against those blue eyes. It is the closest she has come to seeing herself for what she really is, a tired thirty-one-year-old with a lost womb and a vacant sense of self. Seeing that plastic womb and a body bag has reminded her of her place in the world.

Later they lie in bed at opposite sides of the room and listen to each other breathe. Rita stares up at the cracks in the ceiling and thinks of all of the letters she has received in sympathy, the women who have spent months searching in vain for her womb. Above all she remembers a note from a man about being good to her, but knows that without her womb a fulfilling life is no longer possible.

"What's the last thing you'd like to do," Rita asks Adele in a low voice, "before we turn ourselves in?"

She knows Adele will not be surprised that she's decided to surrender, that they cannot get away from finding George and Leonard and facing up to Nodderman, no matter how hard they try. They are women, after all, she thinks, and having men in their lives is par for the course. She hears Adele take in a long, slow breath, as if she's given all she has to finding her answer.

"I'd like a tuna sandwich," she says, and they both start to giggle uncontrollably, their bodies shaking with laughter. They do not stop, in fact, when the policeman bangs on the front door and finds them there, hanging off their beds and kicking their bare feet in the air. In a last moment of rebellion Rita hurls one of her red heels in the air, striking the policeman in the face. It wasn't that she meant to hit him, she says, but the desire to fling off the reminders of her past life got the best of her.

At the police station the reporters crowd the women into the foyer of the station house. Rita sits at a table with the head detective, who shows her snapshots of George lying naked outside the *Nodderman* studio with drawings of his penis stuck to the fenders of nearby cars.

In another photograph she sees him standing in their bare living room with a pair of red heels clutched over his heart. The detective offers her a handkerchief and then blows his own nose. Rita thinks the suffering seems to go on forever among men and women alike.

"I can only imagine what this man has been through," he says with tears in his eyes, "with you losing your womb and leaving him for Nodderman."

Rita says nothing, just nods and stares at the photographs. She wants to say that it wasn't Nodderman she was after at all, but some recognition that her womb was worth mourning. Only after it was gone, she thinks, has she been able to realize just how much grief it brought her. She realizes the man is a detective, however, and that he can probably see these things for himself.

She holds up a photo of a woman with a trail of blood behind her and a dog's carcass lying at her feet. In the woman's eyes she can see the despair at having been driven to such a state on account of a lost womb, suffering because of Rita's misgivings about childbearing.

"Is this woman one of you?" the detective says, as if he is sniffing out hints of a conspiracy.

Rita lifts one of her bare feet in the air and massages

her ankles. She feels the relief at having finally rid herself of the red heels.

"In a sense," she says, but even she is not sure.

The detective takes a long swallow of his coffee and narrows his eyes at her. When he is finished questioning her, Rita searches the crowd of reporters for Adele, but the flashing bulbs prevent her from seeing. Toward the back of the station she sees Nodderman adjusting his glasses and smiling for the cameras. For a moment she thinks of her very first appearance on his show, the shiny white hair and the way he'd pressed his fingers into the stroller mark across her hand. How she'd thought she could count on a man like him to help her get her womb back, but now she sees that even he cannot feel a woman's pain enough to do something about it, no matter how high his television ratings might be.

On the way back to the detective's office, where she is to give a written statement of her life on the lam, Rita hears Nodderman's voice above the calls of the other reporters.

"Hey, Rita," he says, with a glint in his eye, "what would you say if I told you I found your womb?"

There is a long silence, and then Rita's voice, clear and controlled across the station floor.

"I would ask you," she says, looking over at the reporters, who all have erections twitching in their pants, "if you would please give it back to me."

The detective leads her into his office and she sits there for a long time staring at the blank sheets of paper where she is supposed to write her account of her lost womb and the problems that ensued. After all that has happened, she thinks with a wry smile, it's gotten harder and harder to know where to begin.

Although it has been explained to her that she is not really a fugitive, Rita cannot seem to stop feeling like a criminal. Seeing the photos of the dead hemophiliac has riddled her with doubts about her own sense of morality. How does it appear in the eyes of the law, she wonders, not only to have lost her uterus, but to have left *The Nodderman Show* before the end of a taping? She asks the detective if he would like to handcuff her once they are inside his office, but he tells her that won't be necessary.

"Losing a womb is no crime," the detective says in a flat voice. "It's one of life's tragedies, pure and simple."

Still, she cannot stop herself from trying the cuffs on when he excuses himself to go to the men's room.

He leaves her there to write her statement in longhand and offers her a stack of number 2 pencils with long pink erasers. She slides her wrists into the handcuffs and begins to write whatever comes to mind, although her handwriting is cramped and narrow, her wrists aching with the effort.

LOST WOMB:
A STATEMENT GIVEN BY RITA,
A THIRTY-ONE-YEAR-OLD
WOMBLESS WOMAN

I lost my womb some time in the early afternoon of a Wednesday, I believe, outside Reynolds' Shoes. Since that time my life has been a series of mishaps. I have no longer been myself. The lost womb started a frenzy among other women, married and single, young and old. I am responsible for this, I believe. It is my own carelessness that has been my undoing.

Shortly after meeting Nodderman and appearing on his show I began to feel some confidence that the womb would return. Now that, too, is gone. I count among the victims of this tragedy my husband George, my friend Adele, her boyfriend Leonard, a woman named Lucy and her now deceased dog, and a young hemophiliac man I have never met but who took his life with a plastic replica of my womb tied around his neck. I extend my apologies also to Mr. Nodderman and his television audience, as well as to a man who has written to me with promises of being good to me. I submit this statement to the police, who I hope will not stop looking for my womb. A womb, after all is said and done, is a terrible thing to lose.

X

Rita

When the detective returns Rita smiles at him and holds her handcuffed wrists up for him to see. He pleads with her to let him release her, but she insists on keeping them on. The cuffs, she says, are a reminder of her bondage as a woman. As a detective, she says, he should know that better than anyone.

NINETEEN

Down the hall Adele sits in a sergeant's office waiting for a glimpse of Nodderman. She realizes that he is not the man she once thought he was, but still she cannot stop her heart from racing when she sees him in the crowd of reporters. Spending time with Rita in the motel room has made her think differently about her life. For the first time in years she does not feel the overwhelming desire to watch television and even manages to listen to the *Nodderman* theme song without feeling aroused. Her sealed vagina has brought a depth to her life that she had not known before. She is no longer content to watch talk shows and have sex. She will never fall in love with a carpenter like Leonard again. Now she wants more than anything to have her vagina back so she can decide whether or not to let Nodderman in. Entry into her vagina is now a matter of grave concern to all men.

"Before that womb disappeared," she tells the sergeant, "Nodderman was just a dream."

The sergeant nods, types her statement with a clicking of the typewriter keys. Adele tells him she feels better being paraphrased than to write the statement herself. With Nodderman so close by she does not feel she can express herself in her own words.

"By now," she says with a sigh, "everyone must know how I feel."

She begins by telling him about Harry and her fear of his erections, and the love affair with Leonard in front of the television screen. It does not begin to tell the whole story, she says, to explain how her vagina closed up that day. She'll leave that part to Rita.

"Now that she's lived without a womb," she says, "I believe she speaks for us all."

The sergeant asks her what information she can offer him about Lucy, the woman who has not stopped bleeding since their disappearance. Is she somehow connected to this whole scenario, he asks, or is she just a hapless victim of too much television? Adele looks at the photograph of the dead dog and sighs heavily. She thinks about Leonard and his drill, the flakes of her vagina that flew around her apartment. There are no longer any easy answers.

"Maybe Nodderman will know," she says finally. "I've been through too much to tell."

Finally the sergeant agrees to let her go, with the promise that she will contact him if she has any more answers for him. She agrees, although she does not have a forwarding address and telephone number. With any luck at all she hopes to be staying with Nodderman, she says, even though she knows Rita will not approve.

"If that womb is not coming back," she says, "maybe I can at least get my vagina unstuck."

The sergeant wishes her luck and holds the door open for her. Nodderman is waiting for her behind a throng of reporters, but Rita is nowhere to be seen. As she makes her way through the crowd, she sees Rita being photographed in a pair of handcuffs. She tries to run to her and explain that there's no reason for her to be punished, but Nodderman pulls at her arm and forces her to look away.

"What about Rita?" she says, but Nodderman doesn't answer. He leads her out to his limousine and holds out a box tied with a red ribbon.

For a moment she thinks that maybe the womb will be inside, that she'll lift the lid and find it there pink and shining, and her vagina will burst open. But inside she finds a collar belonging to the dead dog, the leather strap worn at the seams.

"Here's to a new life," he says.

She gets inside the limousine and says nothing when he closes the door. All at once he begins to stroke her with his pale hands, his white hair shining against the leather seats. Over and over she feels him pressing against her, as if by some magic he could force his way in. But her vagina remains closed, even after he screams the strains of the theme song in her ear.

TWENTY

This is not at all the way Lucy remembers it. She is reading the statements given to police by both Adele and Rita in the detective's office. Rita was the one who lost her womb, and perhaps should not remain entirely blameless. After all, it is not Rita or Adele who continues to leave a trail of blood everywhere she goes. It is easier for them to fabricate. Her own life, she says, has been laid out like a track.

The detective tells her that Rita has insisted on being kept in a jail cell like a common criminal, although they have not charged her with any crime. The Fruitless Wombs have kept a vigil outside the station house and refuse to leave until the womb is finally recovered. The suffering, they say, must end. Perhaps Lucy should take this into account, he says.

"When that womb was lost, it affected us all," he says with a sigh.

Lucy wipes at her eyes and shakes her head at the detective. How can he expect to understand what it means to be a woman in a world where wombs are lost like old slippers? No man can know that kind of agony. She thinks of poor sweet Sophia lying in the piles of newspaper. Her heart goes out to Rita, she says, but she has her own life to consider. If the womb hadn't been lost in the first place, her own dog might very well be alive today.

"If only she'd been more careful," she says, her voice shaking. "After all, my dog is never coming back. Her womb may turn up."

The detective offers to let her see Rita and speak her piece, but Lucy refuses. All she wants is to get back to her apartment and wait for the bleeding to stop, to hope Nodderman has not yet given up. When she stands to leave, the seat of her pants is soaked with the blood. She tries to wipe it away with the palms of her hands, but instead her palms fill with blood, like stigmata. On her way out the door she leaves a thick red handprint on the white wall, as if to remind him not to forget her. She likes the way it looks there, her handprint staining the pure whiteness of the station walls. She thinks of leaving new messages on the answering machines of her former lovers. In a breathy voice, she will tell them that she has learned to live without a ringing telephone. It took the loss of her dog to teach her what it means to be whole.

She walks home slowly, letting her red heels click on the sidewalk, the blood trailing behind. A group of dogs follow her to her front steps and bark wildly when she tries to go inside.

"There, there," she says, patting their heads.

She leaves them on the doorstep, wagging their tails and lapping at the blood that lies smeared down the steps and into the lingering cracks in the sidewalk.

TWENTY-ONE

In her jail cell Rita dreams that she is pregnant. Her stomach becomes huge, with dark streaks running down like drips of purple candle wax. She is not sure who the father is, although she suspects Nodderman of having had his way with her. There are white hairs over her belly and inside her underpants.

"You white-haired men are all alike," she says with disgust.

The detective comes in dressed as a doctor. He is very convincing, she thinks, with his green gown and a stethoscope dangling around his neck. She lies on the floor with her handcuffs on and spreads her legs in labor. The pains are so sharp that she feels them right up into her throat. Her stomach heaves under her white blouse.

"I think it's coming," she says, but the doctor/detective just stands there with his arms folded. He does not even approach her when she begins to scream.

"Can't you see I'm in pain?" she says, but he just smiles at her and shrugs his shoulders.

The baby comes splashing out of her and lands on the concrete floor with a thud. She can hear Nodderman applauding, his white hair standing on end. The baby lies on the floor without moving. Before she can even pick it up she can tell that it is dead. It is then that she finds George hiding in the corner with his mouth open, tears running down his face and long infant shrieks coming from his throat. She tries to unlock the handcuffs to comfort him, but the wailing keeps on, muffled only by the sound of her handcuffs scraping over the concrete floor.

When she wakes up she asks the detective for a bowl of cereal. She has not wanted one in so long, she says, but the dream has made her throat yearn for the pure coolness of milk. She'd prefer Cheerios, she says, but any kind of cereal will do.

"It's what got me through the whole ordeal," she tells him with a shy smile.

She asks the detective if he wouldn't mind sitting with her while she eats. It's been a long time, she tells him, since she wanted a man around. Since her flight from *The Nodderman Show* she has scarcely thought of George and wonders if the womb was the only thing that kept them together. After his erections disappeared he took to his art like a bat out of hell. "All he wanted to do was draw pictures of his once thriving penis," she says. The thought is enough to make her chuckle, but she fights the urge to do so.

"It just shows you what you can learn to do without," she says, and the detective nods, scribbling notes on his legal pad as if he is taking dictation.

When she is almost finished with the cereal she stares at the milk at the bottom of the bowl. The detective looks at her with hunger in his eyes, the crotch of his pants straining at the zipper. For a moment she wonders if he wants to make love to her, but then she decides it's only the milk he's after, like most men.

Without a word she offers him the bowl and watches as he tilts his neck back to drink, the way his Adam's apple bobs with pleasure. She lays a cuffed hand on his thigh and listens as the milk gurgles in his throat. There are so few things in life that bring her peace these days, she thinks. She has to take these moments as they come.

That night the detective comes to her cell and raps at the bars with his nightstick. Rita sits up straight in her cot, her long hair still curled in the back from all these months of tying it in a bun. For the first time in weeks she feels undone, as if she's been found without a chance to put on her red heels and give her best smile for the camera. She rubs her bare feet against the concrete floor.

"What is it?" she says, feeling her heart beat heavily in her chest, the normally dull thump moving faster and faster. It's as if she knows what he is going to say before he can even get the words out.

"Somebody's found your womb," he says in a whisper. "This time it's the real thing."

When he unlocks the handcuffs she feels only the relief of having her wrists free again. She shakes her hands out to bring some feeling back in them, to end the pins and needles. "The thing about numbness," she tells the detective, "is that you only become aware of it when the sensations come flooding back. You don't realize how long it's been since you've felt things. "

The detective nods. Together they walk down the long hallway leading to the door marked EVIDENCE in careful black letters. It is only when the detective reaches for her hand, when his fingers wrap around hers, that she realizes that the stroller mark on her hand has nearly disappeared.

WOMB FOUND AFTER THREE MONTHS AT LARGE!
WOMEN EVERYWHERE REJOICE!

In an ironic twist, the womb reported missing nearly three months ago by a woman on *The Nodderman Show* was found today in the mall parking lot. The womb was said to be found by a six-year-old girl and her unwed mother on their way home from the shopping mall.

According to the woman, it was her young daughter, Ruth, who was responsible for finding the womb.

The two had spent the day shopping at the mall and were about to return home when the girl stopped her mother from slamming her car in reverse and running over the now famous womb. "If it weren't for Ruthie," she told reporters, "I'd have squashed it for sure." The womb was described as being pink and round with several dents on its sides and around the middle. Police say there is no telling what kind of trauma the womb has endured until it is examined by a group of gynecologists and by Rita, its owner.

Rita, who made her debut on *The Nodderman Show* with her poignant story, is said to be resting comfortably at the county jail, where she now resides. Although Rita could not be reached for comment, Mr. Rod Nodderman issued a statement on behalf of Rita and the other afflicted women, known to the public as Adele and Lucy.

"The womb is home," Nodderman said in a brief statement. "Let us see where this leaves the rest of us."

It is not yet known whether the vagina of one of the afflicted women has reopened or whether Lucy's bleeding has finally stopped. In a gesture of homage, a group of women known as the Fruitless Wombs proclaimed this day as a reminder to all women to never forget what little control they have over their own bodies. When asked why the womb had not been found when it was right there in the parking lot all the time, the former head of security (a man who would identify himself only as Harry) had this to say:

"It seems we were looking in all the wrong places. May God forgive us."

Police have encouraged women to continue shopping at the local mall and to stop worrying for the safety of their wombs. "The mall is not a threatening place," one of the lieutenants said, but local women say they can no longer be too cautious.

TWENTY-TWO

Adele and Nodderman are attempting to make love when they hear the news. Nodderman is poised above her with the top of his white head pressed against her creaseless vagina when the phone rings. It is Nodderman's private line, the one reserved for his producer and for a handful of associates with the show. When it rings, he tells Adele, while banging against her vagina with the top of his head, there is instant cause for alarm.

"Hello?" he breathes into the phone. The hair on the top of his head is matted and pressed into thick clumps. Adele leans back on her elbows to watch him.

Nodderman with his white hair against her sealed vagina is a grave sight, she thinks. Even Leonard was not as persistent, with his drills and plastic goggles. *Leonard did not have Nodderman's finesse,* she observes, *but there was an endearing urgency about him.* In retrospect she thinks that Leonard may even have been charming had she taken the time to notice.

Nodderman clasps the phone to his ear and lets out a long whoop. In a reflex she reaches down between her legs to see if her vagina has reopened. What else could bring such excitement? But with a cursory brush of her fingers she finds it is sealed just as smoothly as that day she and Leonard first caught a glimpse of Rita on television.

What a day that was. She remembers lying on the bed in her crotchless teddy with Nodderman's face looming large on the screen. And now here she is in his television mansion with his life-size presence in this very room. Who would have known what a difference a day makes, she muses. She thinks of Rita handcuffed in her cell in a white T-shirt, of the black body bag that held the hemophiliac's corpse. What does Nodderman make of all this? At times she finds herself wondering, but always there is the proximity of the telephone or his head banging against her that keep her from asking such a question.

Nodderman puts the phone down and grabs her by the upper arms. He is breathing heavily, his chest moving quickly with shallow breaths. She can feel his excitement, the glint in his blue eyes and the way his white hair stands up on end. Slowly, deliberately, she removes his glasses to look directly into the sharp blue eyes. Even as she does it, holding the horn-rimmed glasses in her fingertips, she can feel that the moment is one she will remember for a long time. She has to stop herself from glancing over her shoulder to make sure that there is no cameraman behind them, so intense is her feeling that they are being filmed.

"They've got it back," he says, pulling her to him. He buries his face against her breasts, the smooth white hair prickling the soft skin of her nipples. The sensation is vaguely erotic, but not enough to send her vagina flying open again. She is, she thinks to herself as she cradles Nodderman's head against her breasts, essentially unchanged by the news.

In a flurry of activity they gather up Nodderman's microphone and make-up kit, and the crotchless red teddy she has been saving for such an occasion. They race toward the limousine, their hair flying back, the sound of her red heels hitting the pavement with strong purposeful movements. She cannot remember feeling this excited since she ran away with Rita, and spent long nights eating bonbons and telling each other horror stories of childbirth they'd both heard.

"Just imagine yourself opening," Rita had said, shoving another bonbon into her mouth, "everything that you are splitting open to allow another person into the world. What's left of you after something like that?" Adele knew she did not expect an answer.

Inside the limousine Adele grips Nodderman's hand and opens the window, letting her hair blow straight back and whip him in the face. He does not seem to mind, though, and just brushes the hair absently from his face.

"Let me tell you a story," she says to Nodderman, and proceeds to tell him something Rita had told her the night the hemophiliac was found dead. It is a story of a woman who gave birth on her bathroom floor while waiting for the ambulance. She had no husband at home at the time, and was forced to lay the baby in a copy of *The New York Times* until help arrived. When she was later asked if she'd been scared, the woman said that what kept her going was this: the sight of her huge vagina opening like a mouth and the baby smeared with bits of the sports section. On her belly were figures from the Dow Jones, she said, and a picture of the smiling mayor was pressed on her bathroom floor.

She knew that she was not the only woman in the world, you see, Adele explains to Nodderman. It was that knowledge that kept her going. Surely even he could imagine what that was like.

TWENTY-THREE

Harry and Marty are at a local bar drinking gin and tonics and talking about women's shoes. It is the only safe subject left, one of the men in the bar observes. The women in the world have seen to that, if nothing else.

Harry leans against the bar stool and watches the television that is playing on the other side of the room. Through the smoke and the noise of the jukebox he cannot make out what the reporter is saying, but at this point he doesn't have to hear the words. They are on everybody's lips, no matter how hard they try not to say them.

"They've got that womb," the bartender says, pouring Harry another drink. "The one from *The Nodderman Show.*"

He just nods and listens as Marty goes on about taking inventory at the shoe store. Never in his life, he says, has he seen such a frenzy over women's pumps. He was even caught up in the rush of it himself, he says, shaking his head in disbelief.

"I even fantasized about your girlfriend," Marty says, his face reddening in embarrassment. "With all due respect, of course. Those creaseless jeans were a sight for sore eyes."

Harry takes a long sip of his drink and wonders whether Adele's vagina has unsealed itself. When he thinks back to the nights when she first began to have nightmares about his erection, it comes to him in a series of blurred images. Maybe the vagina had been sealed all along, he thinks, trying to remember the sensation of being inside her. But he can no longer get an erection, no matter how hard he tries, and prefers to spend his nights writing letters and watching the cable channel. At night he can still see Rita's face on the television screen even after the picture is turned off.

Sometimes he falls asleep thinking that she is in the room with him, her dented womb lying in the corner of his bedroom, covered with gravel and hidden under his mall security hat. He wakes up in a cold sweat.

"Well," Marty says, slapping Harry on the back, "I finally feel like a real man again. But I may have to give up selling shoes."

Harry nods, looks around at the other men in their tweed suits with fertile young women hanging on their arms. They all seem to look like Nodderman, he thinks, even though none of the men have white hair. Even Marty with his solid tie and oxford shirt—even he has the aura of television around him. But Harry knows where he belongs in the world, that even without his job and without the woman of his dreams, he is the one who will fight off the old men who lurk outside shoe stores, jerking off in the shadows. Someone has got to do it, after all.

"See you at the mall," Marty calls on his way out the door. For a moment Harry is tempted to follow him, and even stands at the door watching Marty swagger down the street, his arms moving, as if he hasn't got a care in the world. It is as if the womb put a spell on him, he'd told Harry, and now that it's back he can go on living.

I wish it were that easy, Harry thinks.

He stands at the bar and takes his time counting out the money for his tab. Slowly he smooths each bill, creases each dollar so that the face on the front is folded neatly in half. As he is laying out the last bill he notices the thick lines of his ballpoint pen on the back of a dollar bill. *I could have been good to you,* it says under Washington's face, *if only you'd let me.*

TWENTY-FOUR

Rita and the detective are holding hands when the team of gynecologists arrive. They have agreed to examine the womb in Rita's jail cell, which she has decorated with white frilly curtains and a large banner that reads *Welcome Home*. The conditions in a jail cell are far from ideal, one doctor observes, but Rita insists that they look at the womb under her own roof, which, she says, now happens to be in the county jail.

"I want my womb and me to be at home," she says. "After all we've been through, it is the least we can ask."

Rita watches as one gynecologist lifts the womb in his hands and holds it up to the light. In the dim light from the 60-watt bulb that hangs overhead, it is amazing what she is able to see. There in the tiny pink shape she sees the dents that have given the womb an odd curvature around its middle, the once-furious pink now dulled to a dusky rose. The detective squeezes her hand, the handcuffs pressing against her thigh. She can see traces of blood around the sides of the womb and at its pale center. Someone has gotten to it, she realizes, before she's had a chance to fill it.

The gynecologist clears his throat and makes several notes on an oversize clipboard. The other doctors nod at him and pat him on the arm as if to offer him encouragement.

"It would appear," the doctor says, leaning on every word, "that this womb has been used by another woman. There is evidence of pregnancy in every aspect of its shape."

The detective reaches for his holster as if to shoot the team of gynecologists. Rita pulls him by the arm and wraps her arms around his neck. She holds him to her, feels the stubble of his cheek against her face, the stab of his erection at her hip. She has found the right man, she thinks, and no longer has a womb to satisfy him.

"Detective," she says, holding out her wrists for him to handcuff her again, "it just wasn't meant to be."

After several minutes the gynecologists begin to detail the procedure for reinserting the womb. They are not quite sure how it got out, they say, but if it got out at all it is certain to get back in. They will need better lighting and a long metal table for Rita to lie on. Rita merely nods her head and gazes at the detective, whose face is in shadow because of the dimness of the light. She smiles as he tucks the handcuffs away in his shirt pocket. There's no need for that anymore, he tells her. Living without a womb has been punishment enough.

In a calm voice Rita tells the gynecologists that she has decided to take the womb and get on with her life. Now that it's been used, she says, she can start living without guilt. She doesn't need to have it put back in, she says. In fact, she's rather gotten used to being without it.

"Apparently another woman has put it to good use," she tells them, slipping on her red heels and turning to walk out the door. She lifts the womb in her hand and carries it out into the hallway, cradling it in her palms. The detective walks her to the door and offers to give her a ride home, but she tells him that it won't be necessary, since she has no other home to go to.

"I'll leave the light on for you," he says, smiling.

They stand out in the sunlight just looking at each other. What kind blue eyes he has, she thinks, remembering her first glimpse of Nodderman on the day of her appearance. You could almost feel that he understood.

She kisses him in the parking lot and climbs inside her car. Carefully she places the womb on the passenger seat and turns the key in the ignition. The engine starts with a loud whir, the sunlight throwing the colors of the womb all over the car—pink, red, brilliant shades of violet. She waves to him and pulls out of the parking lot, the womb bouncing in the seat next to her.

"I could have been good to you," the detective says in a whisper. But she only hears the rush of the wind through the car window and the scrape of her red heels pushing against the gas pedal with all her might.

TWENTY-FIVE

Several months later Adele announces her pregnancy on *The Nodderman Show*. It seems that one night during a taping her vagina was swept open by the sheer excitement of a live broadcast. Lucy has joined the panel of well-wishers on the show; she is pleased to announce she has not had her period in quite some time. Although she would like to have a child of her own one day, she tells the audience, she has satisfied herself with raising Labrador pups and donating money to pet organizations in the name of her late dog, Sophia, who perished during the womb scare.

"I'll never forget the sight of her lying on my living room rug in a pool of my blood," she says, fighting back tears. "But thanks to the love of Nodderman and his audience, I have managed to live a normal life."

Adele and Nodderman hold hands and smile for the camera. Her waist has begun to thicken a bit, she notices, since she can no longer fit into the crotchless teddies she was once so fond of. Nowadays she spends her days eating bonbons and watching childbirth videos in between tapings of *Nodderman* segments.

"You never know what it means to be having a child," she says, "until it's right there inside of you."

Nodderman squeezes her hand and runs into the audience, holding out his microphone. He heads straight to the back row, where a man is sitting with a box of Cheerios in his lap and a worn security cap pulled over his eyes. The man takes the microphone from Nodderman's hand and breathes into it, his breath rattling through the sound system.

"Do you ever hear from Rita?" he says, his voice barely a whisper over the rumblings of the rest of the audience.

Adele leans back in her seat on the stage and smiles. It is Harry, she knows, even though she cannot see his face in the glare of the stage lights. She thinks of how she once dreaded his erections, about her life with Leonard and the way he'd tried to drill his way inside her. She wants to tell him how often she thinks of Rita and the first day she saw her face on the television screen, about the way her vagina sealed itself shut during a broadcast. How often she remembers the nights at the motel and Rita's stories about childbirth, how they'd both worn red heels and eaten bonbons. The shock of the sirens the night they'd watched the hemophiliac carried out in a long black bag. Sometimes she gets postcards but never with a return address. *The womb is fine,* they say in careful black ink. *Be good to yourself.*

But she knows she cannot say any of this to Harry and instead takes a deep breath and answers the only way she knows how.

"No, I don't," she says with a sad smile. "How are things at the mall?"

Nodderman signals to her that it is time for a commercial. She nods, removing the microphone from her lapel. Lucy tells her about a story she heard recently about Rita involving a search for the perfect pair of shoes.

"They say she does nothing but eat eggs and tell stories about wanting to open up a shoe store," Lucy says in a stage whisper, "but that she'll never set foot in a mall again."

Adele nods, pressing her hands into her swollen white belly. They could all do with a little less of the mall in their lives, she thinks. If nothing else, Rita has surely taught them that.

TWENTY-SIX

At the end of his shift one day, the detective gets a call about a break-in at the shoe store. Normally a man in his position is not called upon to investigate cases of petty theft, but today the precinct is buzzing with activity. The reunion show on *Nodderman* has sparked a local fervor among the towns-people; even his fellow police officers have been glued to their television sets all day.

The chief of police assembles the officers in the briefing room to prepare them for the frenzy that may very well erupt.

"Men," the chief says, looking straight at the detective, "we cannot afford another lost womb in this town. After a *Nodderman* show like this, there's no telling what may happen."

The detective nods and takes a large gulp of his coffee. Just the mention of Rita gives him a yearning for Cheerios, though he has become strictly a Raisin Bran man since her departure. He can still see her standing there in the sunlight with her dented womb on the front seat. How she sped off and left him waving in the distance, the cloud of exhaust bringing tears to his eyes. He feels a tingling in the crotch of his pants just at the thought.

The chief calls the detective aside and whispers in his ear. "Head on over to the shoe store," the chief says, his lips nearly touching the detective's ear, "but for God's sake don't run over any wombs."

The detective tips his hat and feels an urge to click his heels in salute, but stifles himself before it is too late. He walks past the other officers, all hunched over in their seats with their hands on their zippers. The light from the television throws an odd glow over everything, even his badge. From the corner of his eye he can see the sheen of Nodderman's hair gleaming from the television, but he forces himself not to look. She's no longer there, he tells himself. She and her womb are gone for good.

At the shoe store a man named Marty gives him a full account of the break-in. He was taking a late lunch, he tells the detective, and decided to go for a stroll around the mall.

"This mall has meant a great deal to me," Marty says, his eyes shining. "After all that's happened here."

The detective nods, making notes on his yellow lined legal pad. The kind of pad on which he once drew composite pictures of Rita's womb in varying stages of distress, the same pad where she scrawled her deposition with a number 2 pencil. It is difficult to think clearly when his mind is clouded with memories of Rita. Still, he presses on, as only a good cop would do.

Marty leads the detective into the store. Glass from the window has been shattered; everywhere he looks there are open shoe boxes, and tissue paper strewn in all directions. The detective takes notes on all of this and turns to Marty, whose breath, he notices, smells distinctly of tuna fish.

"How many pairs of shoes are missing?" the detective asks, holding his pen poised above the paper in anticipation of Marty's response.

Marty picks up one of the scattered pieces of tissue and blows his nose with it, a gesture which the detective finds oddly poignant, given the seriousness of the destruction. He leans closer to the detective and shakes his head.

"That's just it," he says, his voice barely a whisper. "They haven't taken anything." He takes a deep breath. "They've just destroyed all of the shoes."

The detective raises his eyebrows as he has been trained to do. It is important to maintain a believable amount of concern, the chief once told him, even when your mind wanders. Let them think you hear everything they're saying, he tells himself. Even though all he can think about are wombs.

Marty lifts up one of the broken shoes for the detective to see. The sole of the shoe remains intact, the red patent leather still smooth, uncreased. But the heel of the shoe has been torn off completely, leaving only holes and a round slab of glue where the heel had been.

"They came charging in after *The Nodderman Show*," Marty says. "These women have had enough."

Afterward the detective walks through the rest of the store, taking note of the torn boxes and stubbed heels that litter the floor. Occasionally he lifts a piece of tissue from one of the boxes and presses it to his nose, sniffing. What does a womb smell like? he wonders. He imagines it smells very much like shoes.

When there is no room left on his legal pad, the detective shakes Marty's hand and thanks him for his cooperation. There may be other outbursts, he tells Marty. The mall has seen its share of grief. For now, though, he says, there is nothing to do but look to Nodderman for answers.

"After all that's happened," he says, patting Marty's arm, "Nodderman will know what to do."

He turns and walks out of the shoe store, his heels clicking on the floor of the mall. He's always liked a woman in heels, he thinks, but Rita may have changed all that for him. Now when he thinks of her, he will think of her barefoot or in a pair of moccasins. She has cured him of all that.

"Hey, Officer," Marty calls, running up to him just as the detective is nearly out the door, "do you think Rita had anything to do with this?"

He flashes Marty his badge, thinks of Rita's white wrists and the way she handcuffed herself to her cell. The promises he might have made of being good, if only she had stayed.

He smiles at Marty and closes the door behind him without giving him an answer. Let her have some mystery, he thinks. A woman without a womb deserves at least that much.

Out in the parking lot a man lying on the ground tries to sell him a drawing. The man is lying near the bumper of his squad car and holds up a large banner covered with charcoal pencil scrawls. The detective leans down to help the man to his feet, thinking he is drunk, but the man waves him away with his hand.

"Do you want to buy the picture of my life?" the man says, laughing at the detective out of the side of his mouth.

The detective bends down at the knees to get a closer look at the drawing, but the man holds the paper closer to him, preventing the detective from getting a good look. The detective takes a deep breath, notices the man smells distinctly of shoe leather.

"You've got to trust me on this one," the man says, holding out his hand for the detective to pay him. "This drawing has taken everything I've got."

The detective is tired; he rubs his hands over his face and agrees to buy the man's drawing. He is worried about driving at night in the dark, about the possibility of another womb being flattened under a Goodyear tire. He wants nothing more than to go home and watch the cable station and eat his cereal in peace.

"Here's five bucks, pal," the detective says. "Go draw yourself a new life."

As he pulls away he hears the man laughing at him, high-pitched, almost like screaming. At a red light he unrolls the piece of paper, careful not to tear it at the edges. He holds it up to the light and takes in his breath. There against the background of all that whiteness is a man's penis being squashed by a giant high-heeled shoe. On the bottom of the drawing is the man's scratchy handwriting, bigger than life. *I tried to be good*, it says, *and look where it got me.*

TWENTY-SEVEN

Somewhere in the United States, Rita is driving along an open highway with her womb on the passenger's seat. After all these months, the womb has retained much of its original color, though the sun has bleached it a bit and it has become somewhat more dented from being banged around in the car. Twice she has thought of donating it to local museums and once she almost gave it to a woman with seven children whom she met at a shoe store. With seven children, she thought, a woman must know what a womb is really meant for. Still, she decided after all that the womb's place was with her, there on the passenger seat, her constant companion. Even if they never stayed in one place for very long, they always had each other.

She drives through small towns with lots of road space and no shopping malls. Occasionally she checks into a motel that does not offer cable television or even a telephone. At times she wonders what might be showing on *The Nodderman Show*, but even then she resists the impulse. Mostly she and the womb remain in the car, even to sleep. It's best to keep moving, she thinks. She drives barefoot and sings old Helen Reddy songs.

She thinks of Adele often, of the sight of her in those creaseless jeans, the fun they'd had on the run. Once she thought of calling her from a phone booth outside a shoe store. The mannequin in the window wore tight white jeans and red heels, the seams between her legs smooth as silk. She wonders what has become of George, if he has finally forsaken the memory of his once-powerful penis for a more sedate lovemaking, the kind that comes without penetration. In dreams of him he is selling his drawings at a roadside stop, where he tells passersby about the importance of a womb.

"Hold on to it, no matter what the cost," he tells them. "You never know what it means until it's gone."

He draws bright red apples with pastel backgrounds. Women buy his drawings and hang them in their kitchens. It reminds them of the importance of being fruitful, they tell him.

And sometimes she thinks of the detective, of his kind blue eyes and the way he'd massaged her wrists after the handcuffs had come off. The way his eyes had widened when he'd first seen her womb that day, dented and pocked with bits of gravel. Not even the detectives of the world could protect women from the horrors of losing a womb. This is something she tells herself every day.

One day she stops at a diner to write Adele a postcard. She would prefer to write her long confessional letters in a loopy script with long passages about how the colors of her womb swam like a spectrum in her mind, and the thrill of being barefoot. But instead she keeps her messages short and is careful never to give any information about her whereabouts. Nodderman, she knows, is not above snooping in the mail.

In the diner she places her womb in her purse and washes her feet in the ladies' room sink. Since she never wears shoes, the soles of her feet have turned hard and smell like worn leather. She is careful to keep them clean. When she flushes the toilet she cannot stop herself from thinking about the way she'd searched the restrooms at the mall, the fear of hearing her womb landing on the porcelain with a resounding splat. Even with her womb tucked safely in her purse, the fear of losing it never leaves her.

At a booth she sets her womb down beside her and orders a heaping bowl of Cheerios. The waitress jots down her order and stares at the womb for a long time. The lines around the waitress's mouth and nose seem to fade for an instant, and then she smiles, her eyes shining.

"Is that what I think it is?" she whispers to Rita.

Rita lays a protective hand on the womb, and smiles back. She presses a finger to her lips and gives the waitress a knowing wink. The waitress heads back to the counter and returns with Rita's bowl of Cheerios. She sets the bowl on the table and squeezes Rita's hand.

"After you lost that womb," the waitress says, her eyes full of tears, "my life has never been the same."

Rita thanks her for the cereal and pats the woman's hand. She is grateful for women like this waitress who allow her to remain unrecognized, who take pride in her womb but do not attempt to capitalize on it. When men are nearby she hides the womb down the front of her bra or shoved inside a roll of toilet paper. But with women she can relax and let the womb breathe. After all those months out in the cold, Rita thinks she owes the womb at least a bit of freedom.

Rita takes out a pen and postcard and prepares to write to Adele. Just a short note to let her know the womb is safe, she thinks, a quick message of goodwill. Nothing Nodderman can get his hands on. She eats the cereal slowly, thinking of that first day on *The Nodderman Show*, the heat of being under the camera lights. The milk cools her throat, which is parched from the hours of driving in the sun. *Dear Adele*, she begins, her handwriting a bit shaky at first, but then bolder as she feels her throat begin to cool.

When she is finished the waitress asks her if she'd like another bowl of cereal, and she lowers her head to count the money she has left in her pockets. The womb rests safely beside her, the sunlight reflected from the window throwing colors all around them. It is then that she sees it, a shiny white hair stuck to the front of her red blouse. The hair is thick and wiry, the ends curling around her stomach like a threat.

She turns to the waitress and smiles. "No, thank you," she says.

She picks up the womb and places it on her lap, running her fingers along the sides and in the crevices left by the gravel from the parking lot. In all these months of driving, it is the womb that has kept her mind off Nodderman, the ice of his blue eyes and his microphone thrust at her. The blaring of his theme song and the empty promises. If the womb had not come back, perhaps she'd still be living that life, with her feet squeezed into a pair of red heels and her hair tied back in a bun. The emptiness of her life on television for all the world to see.

Slowly she eats the last bits of her cereal and signs her name in large block letters. With her fingers she takes the hair and holds it up for a minute, watching it glint in the light. She holds the hair over the womb, letting the colors dance all around her. Even in the light the hair seems dull, the once silvery sheen now faded into a muted gray. It doesn't shine nearly as much as she remembers. She holds the hair between her fingers and smiles to herself before taking a deep breath and blowing it away.